COFFEE CRIME CAFÉ

Also By Michael Kerr

DI Matt Barnes Series
A REASON TO KILL
LETHAL INTENT
A NEED TO KILL
CHOSEN TO KILL
A PASSION TO KILL
RAISED TO KILL

The Joe Logan Series
AFTERMATH
ATONEMENT
ABSOLUTION
ALLEGIANCE
ABDUCTION

The Laura Scott Series
A DEADLY COMPULSION
THE SIGN OF FEAR

Other Crime Thrillers
DEADLY REPRISAL
DEADLY REQUITAL
BLACK ROCK BAY
A HUNGER WITHIN
THE SNAKE PIT
A DEADLY STATE OF MIND
TAKEN BY FORCE
DARK NEEDS AND EVIL DEEDS
DEADLY OBSESSION

Science Fiction / Horror
WAITING
CLOSE ENCOUNTERS OF THE STRANGE KIND
RE-EMERGENCE

Children's Fiction
Adventures in Otherworld
PART ONE – THE CHALICE OF HOPE
PART TWO – THE FAIRY CROWN

COFFEE CRIME CAFÉ

BY

MICHAEL KERR

Copyright © Michael Kerr 2017

Michael Kerr has asserted his right under the Copyright and Patents Act 1988 to be identified as the Author of this work.

This book is a work of fiction. Names, characters, businesses, places, events and incidents are either the products of the author's imagination or used in a fictitious manner. Any resemblance to actual persons, living or dead, or actual events is purely coincidental.

ISBN 978-1521730867

Introduction

Many readers do not entertain short stories these days. I don't know why that is. Perhaps like lots of stuff they have simply gone out of fashion – the short stories, not the readers.

I regularly write what I like to think of as little gems and put them in a category that I've christened Coffee Break Yarns. I stockpile them in a file and many will most likely never get to see the light of day. But some do. My last anthology was Close Encounters of the Strange Kind, which is a collection of tales featuring witches, vampires, ghosts, demons and many other weird individuals and creatures.

This offering is wholly crime fiction, although a couple have a slightly horrific aspect. Each one included could probably have been stretched to be a novella or full-length novel, and I admit that some of them gave me the inspiration for books that I have since written.

So why do I write shorts? Answer, because it makes a refreshing change from the long haul of a 100,000+ word thriller. If an idea germinates in my mind I'll run with it, and sometimes produce a two or three thousand word story that I like; usually with a twist to its tail.

Short stories are lean, with all the fat cut away and only a handful of characters at most. Every word counts. You have to involve a reader from the first line and keep your foot hard on the pedal as you speedily reach a hopefully surprising and satisfying conclusion.

Should you decide to dip your feet into this pool of exciting, surprising stories, then I hope that you will enjoy the murder, mystery and thrills on offer.

The title of the collection, Coffee Crime Café, comes from a real café situated in a little village with chocolate box thatch roofed cottages and an olde worlde public house. A large duck pond is at the centre of the green, and the gnarled branches of a lofty and ancient oak tree partly overshadow the nearby café. If able to talk, then surely that old tree would have many of its own stories to tell.

As for the café, it is small and snug, and on most days one or two of the retired locals can be found within, sitting on comfortable cushioned chairs and reading books as they sip coffee or tea from white ceramic cups as big as soup bowls. I like to think that they enjoy the work of Agatha Christie, GK Chesterton, or perhaps Arthur Conan Doyle. They do not appear to be readers of the more violent content that many of my yarns contain. Although I should know by now not to judge a book by its cover, as it could quite feasibly be a wolf in sheep's clothing.

Nb: Just a quirky habit of mine to watch out for: some of the stories are set in the USA, and they are written in US English.

The Magic Cottage
Yorkshire Wolds
June, 2017

Contents

THE WISHING WELL	1
SANTA AND THE ELF	8
A LABOUR OF LOVE	14
HITMAN	21
A REASON TO LIVE	26
HAVE A GOOD LIFE	31
THE BEST LAID PLANS	37
A VISIT FROM JIMMY THE FISH	43
MY NAME IS BENNY TAYLOR	46
A NOT SO PURRFECT MURDER	52
HOW WAS YOUR DAY?	58
A LASTING IMPRESSION	64
A BREACH OF TRUST	72
KATHERINE & EDDIE	79
LIKE TAKING CANDY…	83
THE BLACK FEDORA HAT	90
DAY OF RECKONING	100
HELD TO RANSOM	104
SOMETHING VERY STRANGE	110
ALL THAT GLISTENS	123
A HEAVY HEART	129
A TERRIBLE PLACE	135
ABOUT THE AUTHOR	142

THE WISHING WELL

A three-foot long pickaxe handle made of ash wood makes for a very lethal weapon. The first blow across Eric Parker's back felled him like an ox. His face hit the gravel before he could put his free hand out to lessen the impact. He didn't even feel his nose break, or his front teeth shatter.

The small suitcase Eric had been carrying spun up into the air and turned a couple of times before landing and bursting open on the drive to shed its contents. A second blow to his right side cracked two ribs even as his brain began to acknowledge the initial pain.

Eric knew why he'd been assaulted. It was because he was a freakin' idiot and had dug himself into a deep hole. How deep he didn't know, yet, but soon would.

Harry Shand delivered another hard blow, which fractured Eric's right arm, while Ricky Blaine dropped his pickaxe handle and squatted down to put the bricks of banknotes back in the suitcase.

Eric was moaning, spitting out blood and pieces of teeth as he tensed and curled up on his side, expecting further blows to finish him off.

The plan had been simple. He had been in charge of and responsible for the daily take of cash that had been collected from businesses in the East End. Protection money was what it had always been called. It was an added string to Nick Varney's drug, prostitution, gambling and human trafficking empire. Varney was a gangster, pure and simple, and made his money by employing threats and violence if necessary to keep people paying. No one grassed him up, because the fear of what would happen to them or their loved ones kept them in order.

Eric had succumbed to greed. He'd thought that he could rip Nick off and go back up north to Manchester with a couple of hundred grand to set him up. The window of opportunity was there, and so he had gone for it. How Nick had found out about the theft so quickly was a mystery. He should not have called back at the house he rented in Romford to pick up a few things, but had and was now paying the price.

"You still with us, Parker?" Harry said. "Wouldn't want you to croak, yet. The boss said you should live long enough to regret stealing from him, and then die hard."

Harry and Ricky picked Eric up by his wrists and ankles, carried him over to the open boot of a black BMW, and tossed him in.

Less than twenty minutes later they stopped in darkness on the outskirts of a village near Chigwell. Ricky had been brought up in the area and knew of several decent locations to dump a body. He parked the car next to a small duck pond, climbed over a fence and walked through a stand of trees to a meadow that was part of the Hawksworth Estate, which was now just the ruins of a stately manor house standing in a hundred acres of what had once been park land abounding with deer, but was now overgrown and had been up for sale for at least twenty years.

Clearing a circle of weeds and dead leaves and twigs, Ricky used bolt cutters to cut through the steel shackle of a rusted padlock and remove it from the hasp that was affixed to a concrete surround that held an oak cover in place, which he heaved back to disclose the rim of a well. The well was like a tall, brick-built Victorian factory chimney inverted deep into the ground, not rising high above it. Finding a pebble, Ricky dropped it over the edge and smiled as he heard a splash less than two seconds later. The water would be ice-cold, deep, and probably stagnant. This was the perfect place to leave Parker. He would die alone, terrified, and in total darkness.

When Ricky got back to the car, Harry climbed out and unlocked the boot. Parker was conscious, groaning in pain. Ricky told him to get out.

"I can't," Eric whimpered. My arm's bust, and—"

"Get the hell out of there, now," Ricky said. "Unless you want both of your legs broken as well."

Slowly, painfully and awkwardly, Eric managed to haul himself out of the boot. Ricky nodded in the direction of the trees and told him to walk.

"Are you going to…to kill me?" Eric spluttered through his shredded lips as he shambled along.

"What do you think?" Harry said as he pulled a semiautomatic out of a shoulder rig, screwed a silencer onto the end of the barrel and pointed it at the young man, who by the moonlight he could see was now crying.

Eric wanted to just take his chance and make a run for it, but knew that he wouldn't get more than a couple of yards before a bullet in the back brought him down. He didn't want to die; wished that he could turn the clock back and not steal Varney's money. But you can't turn time back one second. It's not like a DVD, there's no rewind button.

When they reached what to Eric looked to be just a round hole in the ground, Ricky told him to stop and sit down with his legs over the edge of it.

"It's a well," Ricky said. "When I was a kid we thought it was a wishing well. We'd throw a penny in and make a stupid wish. They never came true, though. Just take the plunge. If you don't we'll kick you down it."

Eric looked into the black maw. It was death facing him, up close and personal. There was no way he could force himself to drop into it. He froze, and then screamed as the sole of a shoe connected with his spine and he was shunted forward and began to fall.

Ricky and Harry chuckled as they heard the loud splash echoing up to them. The screaming stopped abruptly, and there was no further sound.

"You think he's dead?" Harry said as Ricky replaced the oak lid, attached a new padlock and covered the top of it again to camouflage its existence.

"I don't know and don't care," Ricky said. "We got the money back and sorted him. Job done."

Returning to the car, they headed back to the city. Harry made a call to let Nick Varney know that the problem was resolved, and then they stopped off at the Blind Beggar pub in Whitechapel for a burger and a pint. The place was still infamous, due to Ronnie Kray having shot another gangster, George Cornell, in the head with a Luger pistol, way back in nineteen sixty-six.

Eric hit the water hard, sank, but remained conscious. He had somehow dropped down the well without coming into contact with the brickwork that lined it. Bobbing back to the surface, almost choking on the foul-smelling water, he reached out with his left hand and held on to the rough interior and paddled with his feet to keep afloat. This was it, the end, and the paralysing fear that he felt in the Delphic gloom was all-consuming. A part of him wanted it to be over with; just give up to the inevitable and let go and be done with it, but the survival instinct had kicked in and compelled him to fight for life. He just wished with every fibre of his heart and soul that a miracle would save him.

Cindy Murray heard the scream above the sound of Lionel Ritchie singing on the car radio. She grasped hold of Steve's hand and stopped it from pulling her panties down.

"What's wrong?" Steve Atkins said. "I thought you were in the mood for it."

"I am, love, but didn't you hear that scream?" Cindy said.

"I heard something, but it could've been a sodding owl shrieking."

"It was human, Steve. And it was nearby."

Steve had driven out to the deserted location after they'd had a meal at the Chequers pub in Barkingside. He'd parked the Astra on a lane that was flanked by trees, and opened the window a couple of inches, knowing that things were going to get a little steamy.

Cindy got out of the car and tiptoed over to a gap in the overgrown hedgerow, to see two figures illuminated by the moon. One was standing. The other was knelt down. She could hear them talking, but couldn't make out what they were saying. After no longer than a minute they walked away.

"What?" Steve said, making her jump as he appeared at her side.

"Two guys just buggered off," Cindy said. "We need to go and see what they were up to."

"Why?"

"Because I heard someone scream, that's why."

Steve sighed. His take on life was that ignorance was usually bliss. Trouble was something to avoid, not go looking for.

Cindy forced her way through the bushes, unmindful of scratching her hands and arms on branches and thorns. Steve followed her.

It only took them a minute to find the disturbed patch of ground. Cindy knelt down and clawed the leaves and grass away from what was a large, round wooden cover.

"Now what?" Steve said.

"It's padlocked," Cindy said. "Go and get something to open it with."

Steve made his way to the car, got a wheel brace from the pack in the boot and hurried back with it. It only took him seconds to prise the hasp from the wood. The rusted screws popped out like rotten teeth.

"Hello," Cindy shouted into the well after Steve had raised the cover and dropped it back onto the long grass.

Eric couldn't believe that the darkness had become lighter. Looking up he could see an edge of the moon directly above him. Was this salvation? Was he hallucinating? Or had a female voice just shouted down to him?

"Help me," he shouted back.

"Phone the police and fire brigade," Cindy said to Steve. And he did.

It was a DI by the name of Barnes that interviewed Eric several hours' later in a private room at the Queen's Hospital in Romford, after he had undergone surgery on his fractured arm and had had his other injuries treated.

"So tell me the story," Barnes said. "We know that you worked for Nick Varney, and that you obviously did something to piss him off big-time."

"I'm not a snitch," Eric said. "I've got nothing to say to you."

"You're a marked man, Mr Parker. You know that he'll find out that you're still alive and put a contract out on you. For all we know there could be a shooter in the hospital now. You need to decide which way to jump, and quickly. If I don't get assurances from you, then you're on your own."

It was true, and Eric knew it. He was backed into a corner, and the copper was the only lifeline he could take a chance on, if he didn't want to spend every hour of every day waiting to be double-tapped.

"So what are you offering?" Eric said.

"You give us everything you know, and then back it up in a witness box at the Old Bailey. If we get a conviction against Varney, then you get a change of identity and a new life to live in another part of the country. Take it or leave it."

Eric took it. He wanted to live and so he gave them everything he knew; names, dates, deals and details that could be confirmed and followed up on.

Nick Varney eventually went down for ten years. There was no proof that he had arranged to have people killed, but enough other stuff to get him put away for a reasonable length of time.

Eric got up and watched the sun rise over the River Humber through the bedroom window of his fourth floor flat on St Andrews Quay in Kingston upon Hull. It was the city's Year of Culture, not that he gave a rat's arse. What he *did* care about was the fact that he felt safe. He was now known as Martin Payne, and had a regular job, and could sleep at night, although the near death experience of being down that well would be a recurring nightmare that would haunt him for the rest of his life.

SANTA AND THE ELF

THE pickup truck slid to a skidding stop in thick snow outside the front of the Tree Top Diner, and a big, heavyset guy wearing a matching white-trimmed red suit and hat climbed out the driver's side as a much smaller figure dressed as an elf got out the passenger door. The Santa look-alike adjusted the thick false beard on the mask of Donald Trump, that he was obviously wearing to disguise his features, and the elf realigned the long plastic nose that was held in place with a length of elastic around his head

"You know what to do," Santa said as he walked up the rustic hardwood steps to the entrance door.

"Yeah," Elf said. "Let's get on with it and give these folks a Christmas Eve to remember."

Marty Abbott was short-staffed, which had also made him short-tempered. His cook, Billy, had hit a patch of ice the previous evening, spun off the blacktop and crashed his old Buick into a Ponderosa pine that didn't give so much as an inch. Billy had been lucky, if breaking a leg and his nose could be deemed as such. That didn't help Marty, though. The steaks, burgers, eggs, bacon and a heap of other stuff still had to be flipped, and even reducing the meal availability on the menu didn't cut him a lot of slack. The place was heaving, and even with one of the three waitresses, Caroline, helping him out in the kitchen, customers still had to wait too long for their chow. One or two had already left. Unknowingly, they were the lucky ones.

Santa strode passed the counter and pushed open the door that had a sign saying STAFF ONLY on it, while Elf locked the entrance door and waited in the small foyer.

"Merry Christmas," Santa said, pointing a Glock 17 semiautomatic pistol at the harassed-looking guy who had a mess of food sizzling on a large griddle.

Marty blinked away perspiration that had run down through his eyebrows and into his eyes, and stepped in front of Caroline and said, "What the hell do you want?"

"Money from your safe and cash register. Do anything stupid and my friend out front will start shooting the customers."

Marty dropped the metal flipper he was holding and accepted that he had no choice but to do as he was told. The robber could be bluffing, but he couldn't take the chance. He nodded to the open door of a small office at the rear of the kitchen and said, "The safe is in there."

"So go and get the cash, and leave the door wide open so that I can see you. If I even think that you've activated an alarm, then your hired help here gets a bullet in her pretty little head for starters."

Marty went and got the money and came back with it. The would-be Santa pulled a large folded-up canvas sack from a deep pocket of his costume and tossed it to him. Marty didn't need telling what to do. He opened up the bag and stuffed a couple of blocks of banded bills into it.

"Okay, now let's go out front and finish up," Santa said.

Elf walked through the arch into the diner proper, paused to pull the plug of the Juke to cut off Brenda Lee singing Rockin' Around The Christmas Tree, and sudden silence got everyone's attention.

"Here's the plan, folks," Elf shouted as he waved an AK-47 around the crowded diner. "Santa and the waitress are going to come table to table with a sack. This year we're collecting gifts, not giving them out. Have your wallets, phones and jewelry ready to drop in the sack. And bear in mind that If I see anyone attempting to make a call I'll start shooting. Just do exactly as you're told and you'll live to see Christmas Day."

Santa, known out of costume as Andy Barrett, a small-time thief originally from Kansas City, brought the barrel of the pistol up and across to hit Marty a stunning blow to the temple, followed by another as he crumpled to the floor.

He was leaning forward into a mix of wind, snow and hail that blew almost horizontally into him, stinging his face like splinters of freezing glass. He was a very tall guy, clothed in a greatcoat over a thick plaid shirt and blue jeans. He wore a knitted watch cap pulled down low to cover his ears, and his gloved hands grasped the straps of the rucksack he had on his back.

Through the almost blinding whiteout, Logan saw a faint glow in the distance and smiled. He knew that it was the lights of the Tree Top, a small diner and motel complex. A few more minutes and he would be inside, warming up and anticipating a pot of steaming black coffee and a steak with all the trimmings. You needed to be uncomfortable sometimes, so that you could appreciate the good things when they came your way.

He reached the door and pushed, but it was locked. That didn't make sense. It was only nine p.m. and the car lot was full, and he could see that most of the tables and booths inside the diner were occupied. Looking through the plate glass door he saw some guy not much bigger than a midget, and dressed up like an elf. No problem with that, but the fact that he was wielding a submachine gun, was.

Stepping to the side of the door, Logan kept to the wall and furtively took a quick look through one of the windows. Another guy, taller and dressed up as Santa Claus was going from table to table, and a woman that looked to be a waitress was taking valuables from the tops of them. This was an armed robbery in progress.

Instantly in action mode with adrenaline pumping through him, Logan backed up, turned and made his way around to the rear of the diner, to enter it though an unlocked door that led into a large kitchen. The air was full of smoke, and the stink of burning meat and cooking oil. Without hesitation he pulled off his gloves and selected a large steel steak hammer from one of the hooks hanging from a rack above the central island. Commonsense told him to dig out the phone from his rucksack and call the police. But this place was remote, at least ten miles from the nearest town, and every second counted. If one of the patrons panicked and did something stupid, then the midget in the silly costume could get an itchy trigger finger and turn the diner into a charnel house.

Bending low and making his way out of the kitchen, Logan ducked down behind the counter. The robber with the AK-47 was the main threat. He was standing with his back to the counter, less than three feet away from it, within reach.

Sometimes you just had to go with your instincts and do what needs to be done without too much conscious thought about it. All the danger that Logan had run into up to this moment in his life gave him the confidence to make his move.

Elf: real name Dewey Carter, heard a low whistle come from directly behind him, and instinctively turned his head.
The stake hammer pounded into the top of his skull, leaving a bloody cross-hatched pattern on his scalp. Blood trickled out from the edge of the pointy hat he wore, as his eyes rolled back to show the whites. Even as Dewey fell, Logan grasped the barrel of the rifle and pulled the weapon from slack fingers, to reverse it and aim it at the bogus Santa Claus.

"Drop the firearm, now, and then lay face down on the floor, hands clasped behind your head, or I'll shoot you," Logan said in a clear, menacing tone of voice.

Andy Barrett wondered if he could raise the Glock and get off a shot, but only for less than half a second. The steely look in the big guy's eyes seemed to be talking to him, wanting him to go for broke. He let go of the gun and did what he'd been told to.

"Who are *you*?" Logan said the young woman who was standing next to Santa, wearing a lemon-colored nylon tunic.

"Caroline Maston. I'm a waitress."

"That's the truth," one of the customers said. "I eat here regularly. Caroline has waited on for at least four years."

Another three diners backed that up.

"Best get back to the kitchen and switch everything off," Logan said to Caroline. "The chicken, steak and burgers are cremated. Given any more time the place will probably burn down."

Logan told one of the customers to call 911 for police and an ambulance, and another to go find some duct tape or twine from the kitchen or office, while he picked the Glock up and sat down in a booth with his booted foot on the back of Santa's neck. When Caroline came back he told her that he could use a cup of coffee, strong and black.

It was the small hours' on the morning of Christmas Day when the police finished up interviewing everyone and left. Dewey (the elf) Carter had been taken to A&E in need of treatment for his scalp wound and suffering from concussion. Andy (Santa) Barrett had gone directly to Jail.

Marty Abbott had a force ten headache, having been gun whipped, but refused to go to the hospital. He didn't have double vision and hadn't even thrown up, so let a paramedic put dressings on the two minor wounds.

Caroline had told Marty how Logan had saved the day, so to speak, before she'd phoned her husband, who came to take her home after the police said that she was free to go.

"What's your plan?" Marty said to Logan when just the two of them remained in the diner.

"The police will want to talk to me again. Other than that I don't have much in the way of plans," Logan said. "I go where my feet take me. At this moment in time I'd appreciate some more coffee, a bite to eat, and to stay here till daylight before I go into town."

"That's the least I can do," Marty said. I'll go fix the coffee and make us both a sandwich. And if you want to stay in one of the motel rooms for a couple of days, you're welcome to, on the house."

It ended up being a good Christmas for Logan. He wound up staying at the Tree Top for three days, ate well, and made a new friend in Marty Abbott.

A LABOUR OF LOVE

Whitechapel, London ~ November, 1888.

HE is dressed in black, wears a top hat and walks stiffly, erect, with no destination in mind. He is hunting.

Save for the muted howl of a lone dog bemoaning its chained and wretched existence, there is only the sound of a hissing gaslight fracturing the thick silence of a fog-bound night. The soft light dimly brightens the cobbled street below it. He stops in the yellow glow, reaches into his frock-coat and withdraws a small silver case; flat and heavy. A gloved thumb depresses a stud and the lid springs back to disclose a cache of hand-rolled cigarettes, one of which plucks out to place between thin lips. A struck match flares, and fleeting glimpses of features are revealed. The face is lean, with parchment skin drawn tight over its chiselled planes, and a hooked nose – beak-like – separates deep-set eyes of liquid pitch, which stare emotionless and unblinking. The lurking figure inhales a deep draught of smoke, holds it warm in his lungs, and then releases it slowly into the chill night air. He absently flicks a strand of tobacco from his dimpled, lantern jaw, and waits.

From the dense curtain of polluted, sulphurous fog, a distant sound escapes. Clip...Clip...Clip: the clip of heels on flagstones heralds the approach of another walker abroad in the midst of evening.

The whore appears like a phantom from the murk, drifting towards him as if a doorway had opened in the dense vapour to disgorge her; granting entry to his court.

She slows as she spies the well dressed gent, giving him time to assess her wares. Her bodice is nearly fastened, breasts heaving, pushing up and out to exaggerate and advertise her cleavage. And her gaudy makeup is smudged, with painted ruby lips parted in a crooked smile, as she contemplates more profit for her purse.

"I have a carriage," he states, his cultured voice a soft, deep and roast almond baritone.

She swaggers up, right hand on hip, fluttering her eyelashes in gruesome parody of coyness.

"Well, bein' as yer look like a gen'leman of substance, an' 'ave a carriage no less, an' fine-cut west end clothes to boot...let's see," she said, pausing, catching her bottom lip between decaying teeth as she ponders over what charge to levy. "Three bob I reckon, an' not a penny less to 'ave me raise these skirts on a perishin' night like this."

"Let us agree to a crown and not haggle. I'm sure that you will entertain me well for so much recompense," he said, producing a five shilling piece from his waistcoat and holding it up for her inspection, before returning it to the safety of his pocket.

Lizzy linked her arm through his, now eager to relieve him of his need and from his money with all due alacrity.

"Lead the way, kind sir," she said. "I'll give yer a proper treat, I will. Anyfink yer fancy fer that crown. An' if yer enjoy what yer get tonight, yer jus' might want more of the same on a regular basis."

They walked a few yards back along Tannery Row; the astringent odour of rawhide soaking in tannic acid leaving no doubt as to how the street had earned its name.

"Down here," he said, stepping into the dark maw of Lambert Alley.

The hansom almost blended with the night; black on black; the snorting of a horse the only clue as to its presence.

With little room between cabriolet and wall, they stepped up and climbed into the snug two-seater transport. And as they did, Lizzy saw the glow from the driver's clay pipe. He was sat up high at the rear of the cab, the reins from one hand snaking over the roof to the ebony beast in front. He tipped a finger to his cap, and gave a slight nod of acknowledgement, and what could have been a sly but fleeting smile.

Lizzy Skinner was eighteen, though looked a decade older. She had worked the streets for almost five years, and could neither read nor write; her only education and expertise being a full practical schooling in carnal knowledge. Her father, God rot his wick, had seen to that, having bedded her regularly since she was ten. He had taken off to sea years ago, never to return. Lizzy's mother gave up laundry work and all honest toil at that time, finding that she could make more money and sweat less on her back than she had ever made standing up. Many a night, Lizzy was kept awake by the grunting of her mother's clients, with only a frayed and timeworn curtain dividing the one-room hovel to separate her from the unsightly antics.

Eventually, Lizzy had nursed her mother, and watched her waste away and die of consumption. That had been a year ago, and now she saved every penny that she could, determined to escape the East End and start afresh, away from the city.

She lifted up her skirts, and the vestigial light illuminated her heavy, white thighs, which were unfettered by any undergarments.

He made no sound at all. Not a murmur escaped his lips as he quickly took his pleasure. Finished, he sat back and adjusted his clothing, as Lizzy hastily covered her nether regions and waited.

Withdrawing the gleaming crown, he proffered payment, holding it out to the smiling strumpet. She reached for the coin, and as her fingers grazed its edge it was dropped to the cab's floor. She followed it down, bending low in the cramped space, feeling for it blindly in the darkness. And as she found and grasped her bounty, the man knelt on her back, his knee forcing her face ever nearer to the musty, wooden floor. He gripped her long, raven tresses in his left hand, twisting the hair tightly in his closed fist.

"What's yer game?" Lizzy cried out, angry, and with seeds of fear beginning to germinate in her dull brain.

He pulled her head back, swift and hard, inserting the point of a butcher's knife into her neck, just below the left ear. She took a breath to loose off a scream, but before she could utter a sound he pulled the honed blade deeply across her taut throat, opening arteries and severing her windpipe, cutting with such force and ferocity that the cold steel nicked her vertebrae. Blood erupted in pulsing spurts as her almost decapitated head fell back to face the hansom's ceiling.

Lizzy tasted the blood as it filled her mouth. Her bowels and bladder reneged, voiding themselves noisily as she looked up at a hitherto impossible angle. She heard the choking, gurgling in her open throat, and saw bright motes of incandescent light dancing before her eyes like myriad stars on a black velvet backcloth of night sky. And not one by one, but in perfect unity, they all winked out, and Lizzy crossed the lonely bridge from life into the hereafter.

Jimmy Hudson had been drinking ale at the King's Arms, which was a tavern on Bowley Street. Walking out, well wrapped against the brumous night, he paused to don his woollen mittens before setting off at a swift pace, unable to see more than an arm's length in front of him in air as thick as winter soup. By way of a shortcut he entered Lambert Alley, its narrow passage so choked with yellow smog that he had to feel his way along the damp brick wall. Halfway along, his foot connected with something which spun away, clattering over the cobblestones and arousing his curiosity as to what it might be. He bent down low from the waist (as only the young and supple can), his hands searching inch by inch in the area that he thought the object had come to rest.

Jimmy was seventeen, apprenticed to a butcher and learning his trade well. He still lived with his parents, along with two siblings, both girls. Between them, the Hudson family earned a reasonable income, which enabled them to rent a house a fair distance from the factories and tanning yards, to enjoy a good diet and wear clothing that had not belonged to deceased family members, or been purchased third or fourth hand.

Jimmy was a personable young man, honest as the day is long, and blessed with a carefree attitude to life, that had not yet been diminished by any fearsome blight.

"Ouch!" he exclaimed, coming upon the object with his thumb, pulling back as if pricked by a rose thorn, or nipped by a rat, of which there was an overabundance. He reached out again, gingerly, and explored the shape of his find. It was a knife. Not just any old knife; no common blade, but a butchers tool of fine Sheffield steel with a riveted walnut handle. Finder's keepers, Jimmy thought, examining it closely as he continued on his way. But after only several steps he tripped, to sprawl headlong over a large obstacle, spraining his wrist as he put his hand out to save his face from the cobbles.

Scrambling off the soft heap, he knew instinctively that it was a human being. Heart pounding like a bailiff at the door, he knelt back down and lowered his face to the supine figure, and as if to aid his inspection, the fog swirled and thinned a jot, giving a clear sight of the previously hidden horror. It was a young woman. Her large blue eyes were glazed and set, staring up through him to infinity. Her throat hung wide open, a gaping, clotted gash. And if that were not gruesome enough, then there was more. Spellbound, Jimmy saw that her clothing had been cut away, laid open at the front, and that her breasts had been removed and her stomach rent open to spill her guts out onto the ground. Turning aside as though his looking were causing her further indignity, he vomited, retching until his stomach hurt and his eyes were streaming with tears. At last the spasms passed. He stood up, belching, spitting out sour bile and wiping threads of spittle from his mouth with a coat sleeve.

"Oy, what goes on?" A peeler cried, racing down the alley, his truncheon drawn.

"I...I...found—" Jimmy started, holding forth the knife.

The oak cudgel smashed into his left temple, knocking him senseless, denying him the chance of reasonable explanation.

The result of the subsequent trial was a foregone conclusion. Jimmy had been found next to the victim's body, a bloody weapon in hand and his clothing besmeared. Guilty, was the unanimous verdict of the jury; of murder done with malice; a heinous crime. The judge produced what looked to be a jet-black silk handkerchief and placed it over his powdered wig. At this a hush descended on the courtroom as all present waited with bated breath to hear the passing of the death sentence.

Jimmy had to be held upright as he was informed that he would be hanged by the neck until dead. The judge added that he trusted God would show more compassion to him than he had shown his innocent young victim.

The morning of the execution duly arrived. Jimmy could not eat, and had he not been going to swing, then would most certainly have starved away. His heart was as leaden as his feet as he was led to the topping shed of Wandsworth prison. And on climbing the wooden steps of the scaffold on rubbery legs, he began to cry.

The hangman had weighed and measured the boy to calculate the drop. Too long a drop and the head could be torn from the body; too short and the subject would asphyxiate and suffer a slow demise. It had to be just right, if professional pride was to be maintained. When executed properly, the hapless subject would fall to almost instantaneous death. The neck would break, and the corpse would make a half turn to the right and hang still.

Charles Plimpton was one of several hangmen employed on a regular basis. He would travel in from Woking and dispatch maybe ten condemned men and women during a five day period. The fee was low, considering the infrequency and nature of his trade, and bearing in mind that just one bungled job could put him off the list, out of favour and poorer for it.

Jimmy stood on the trap with difficulty, shaking and in the grip of a terror that crushed his heart in an icy grip as his stomach churned in the manner of a ball of squirming worms fighting to untangle themselves.

The hangman, quick as a fox, secured Jimmy's wrists and ankles with well worn leather straps.

"I di...didn't do it, 'onest, guv," Jimmy said with his eyes awash and face as white as high grade flour.

"I know, son. I know," the executioner replied as he lowered the hood and then tightened the noose around the youngster's neck.

The trap was loosed, and yet another tormented soul dropped through on a swift journey to heaven or hell.

"An unpleasant task well carried out," said Henry Marsh, the prison governor. "Thank you Charles, you always send them off quick and clean."

"It's my pleasure to be of service once again." Charles said, his comment heartfelt and sincere; his work a vocation; a labour of love.

Replacing his top hat, the hangman left the platform with a sparkle in his oil-black eyes and the trace of a smile on his thin-lipped mouth.

"Let me assist," he said in a deep, rich voice as the body was taken down. He was eager to reclaim his straps, hood and rope and be on his way.

As he stepped through the prison's gate, Charles absently rubbed his lantern jaw, and then reached into a pocket for his silver cigarette case.

Late that very evening, again in shrouding fog, the hansom rattled through the cobbled side streets of Whitechapel. It was back to Woking in the morning, and Charles wanted to make the most of his last night in the city.

HITMAN

HE parked in the side lot of the Pumpkin Patch Diner in Flatbush, walked in and sat at a booth across the table from Darnell on an old, faded red vinyl-covered bench seat that had strips of silver duct tape holding what were probably knife cuts together in places. The joint was like a second home to him, with the smell of fried food and coffee in the air and no doubt permeating into the fabric of the walls and ceiling. All that was missing these days was the stink of cigarette and cigar smoke. He had finished his Marlboro before entering, to grind it out on the wet sidewalk with the sole of his boot.

Time moved on, and life changed for better or worse. He preferred things how they'd been back in the late sixties and early seventies, when he'd been a youngster; before all the political correctness came in and everyone swapped real living for a virtual world, to spend most of their sad lives in front of computer monitors and game consoles, messaging, tweeting, and uploading photos of what they'd had for lunch and the like on social media. And even here in the diner at least half of the dummies had cell phones held to their ears and were talking or on the 'net as they ate. 'It's life, Jim, but not as we know it' came to mind from the old Star Trek TV series.

He nodded, and Darnell nodded back. A waitress sidled up to the booth. She was a teenager with bottle-blond hair, almost expressionless bovine eyes, studs in her nose and lips and god knows where else, and she was chewing gum with her mouth open. A plastic name tag pinned to her sweater over her ample left breast identified her as Wanda. What a life. She would probably still be serving burgers and fries here in twenty-five years. Some people had very bleak futures stretching out ahead of them like faded and well-worn carpets. It saddened him in a way to think that the vast majority of folk had no real aspiration. They just worked, paid taxes and then died. Okay, they found time to pump out the next generation, but that didn't take much more than lust to accomplish.

He asked for coffee.

"You got the cash?" Darnell said after Wanda had poured some of the thick black java from a pot into a white ceramic mug and then ambled over to another booth, out of earshot.

"Yeah."

"Good. Pass it to me under the table."

He took his windbreaker off, laid it on the bench and slid a fat envelope out of a side pocket and handed it across under the table, out of sight of anyone.

"So how's it going, Arnie?" Darnell said as he held his own now empty mug up and waved it in the air until Wanda eventually caught the movement, made her way over and refilled it for him.

"It's going just fine," he said. "I've got a Toyota dealership six blocks from here, and a nice house just a fifteen minute drive from Coney Island."

"The American Dream, eh?" Darnell said, staring at Arnie with eyes as gray as Motown steel.

Arnie shrugged and said, "Why do you it?"

"Do what?"

"Kill people."

Darnell smiled, but there was no trace of humor in the expression. "I do it because people like you can't. It beats working my balls off doing a regular job. I'm self-employed and I get paid well to do something that I did as a soldier for a pittance. Blowing rag heads away in Iraq was fun, but I didn't believe for a second that we should have been out there, or that we'd make any worthwhile difference."

Arnie said nothing. He'd known Darnell since high school, and remembered a quiet, reserved young man who had played guitar and dreamed of being in some rock band. But he had not been good enough, and a girl that he'd loved had dumped him and his personality had changed.

"But—"

"No buts or any more questions buddy," Darnell said. "I get a lot of satisfaction out of planning and carrying out a hit. They say that you should stick to what you know, so I do, and being good at it gives me a great deal of fulfillment. Doing what turns you on and also pays well is all you can ask from life."

Arnie nodded. He was as bad if not worse than Darnell, so had no right to be judgmental. He had asked him to murder someone, had taken out the contract, and was wholly responsible for what would happen the following Wednesday evening when he would be three hundred and eighty miles away in Pittsburgh at a Toyota convention.

Julia Brewster had been to an art exhibition with two girlfriends. She had sipped her way through four flutes of champagne and talked at length to a couple of the local artists. One, Tom Sherman, had loosely based his style on the Brit painter, Hockney. He was tall, had craggy good-looks, was in his late thirties, and had all the necessary charm to ensure that he would sell his work.

It was almost midnight when Julia climbed into bed. The house felt empty with Arnie away on business in Pittsburgh. She smiled, snuggled down and drifted into sleep, to dream of being naked in her shower room in the company of Tom Sherman.

At a little after two a.m. Darnell eased open the door and walked across the carpet to the side of the bed. He was holding a Glock 17 semiautomatic pistol fitted with a suppressor in his right hand. The horizontal rays of moonlight through the gaps in the Venetian blind at the window striped everything in the room, and he recognised his mark.

Lifting a plump pillow from next to the sleeping figure, he pressed it firmly against the face and fired the gun into it three times. The body jerked up, back arched as if it had been electrocuted, to go into spasm and then fall back, limp and lifeless.

Darnell lifted the pillow back to check his work. One bullet had gone through the left eye, and the other two had passed through the forehead. It had been a quick kill.

Outside, he removed his gloves as he made his way to where he had parked his car. He felt better than he had done for years…yes, years. Tonight had been personal, and he fully expected that it would modify his life for the better.

Back in Brooklyn at nine a.m., an unmarked Ford pulled up to the detached house on a development off Shore Parkway.

One of the two detectives broke the news. There was no easy way to do it. They just confirmed that she was Julia Brewster and informed her that her husband had been murdered, shot to death in a hotel room in Pittsburgh. They asked her to show them a photo of Arnie, to confirm his identity beyond all doubt, even though they had found his driving license and credit cards in his otherwise empty wallet.

It was done. They asked a few of the usual questions, took a statement and left.

Julia brewed coffee and sat and let the dramatic change in her life sink in. She felt no guilt. Throughout their marriage Arnie had bedded too many women, and had on numerous occasions beaten her when he was drunk, which was often. He had changed from the personable young man that she had fallen in love with back in high school days to become a complete son of a bitch.

And then, just a few days after telling Arnie that she was planning to leave him, she had been approached by Darnell in a deli on Park Street. She hadn't seen him for years, but had always wondered how it might have turned out if she hadn't dumped him for Arnie. He inserted an SD card in a handheld digital voice recorder and played it to her.

There was no ambiguity. Arnie had offered to pay Darnell to kill her, rather than go through a divorce and be hit with a hefty settlement bill.

It was over a month after he had whacked Arnie that Darnell turned up as if by chance to meet Julia in the same deli on Park Street. They ordered sandwiches and coffee and talked about the future, not the past. Darnell asked her out on a date, and she said that would be nice.

It was funny how things worked out, Darnell thought. You never knew what marvelous or dire events where waiting up ahead on life's highway to greet or defeat you.

A REASON TO LIVE

SITTING in a bar in a small town in Idaho getting shit-faced and wearing a shoulder holster with an empty gun in it may seem a funny thing to do, but I'm not laughing. Events have caught up with me and I've got no future worth spit to look forward to. I've been on borrowed time for a while, and now it has almost run out on me. I'm sick of running, always looking over my shoulder and expecting to be whacked. Yeah, I know, I'm paranoid, but only because there's an open contract out on me.

There are probably millions of people that don't believe in coincidence, but they're wrong. I know that for a fact, and not just because of a purely statistical perspective that they are inevitable and are happening all the time. And life only seems to have a semblance of order. Truth is we live in semi-organized chaos, going through each day with an irrational expectancy that we'll survive to carry on doing whatever it is we do as the seconds, minutes and hours of our existence tick by. Okay, I'm sounding a little cynical and dejected and defeated, but so would you if you'd been as stupid as me.

It was over a year now since I'd let Jerry Walker and Al Barrow talk me into the heist. It hadn't taken much persuasion on their part. I was up for it. I'd been laid off from the factory and money was as tight as an old hooker's corset. My girlfriend, Angie, was working long hours' for peanuts at a laundry in the Bronx, and was getting more pissed with every day that passed. Love really can fly out of the window if you spend too much time arguing over unpaid bills. It felt as though we were a road traffic accident waiting to happen. That was when one huge coincidence occurred. After a squabble with Angie I left the apartment and called in at Hoagie's Diner for a cup of coffee. I then walked four blocks south on Southern Boulevard to 183rd Street and made a spur of the moment decision to spend an hour or two at the zoo, which I hadn't visited for twenty years. And I hadn't seen Jerry for fifteen years, since I'd dropped out of high school. And there he was, standing in front of a rail fence with another guy; both of them licking at ice-cream cones as they watched the sea lions get fed. Jerry was wearing a sharp suit and shiny loafers and looked as though life was treating him good. I decided to walk on by, but a rug rat being pushed in a stroller behind me dropped a toy and started screaming its lungs out. Jerry looked around, saw me and headed my way with a big crooked smile on his broad face.

Long story short. They needed a driver. All I had to do was wait for them in a parking lot at the rear of a nightclub in Queens. There was a big stake game scheduled to take place in a private room, and so it would be easy pickings, or so Jerry thought.

They had hit the club after midnight, armed and wearing plastic clown face masks. A couple of minutes later I heard shots as I sat at the wheel with the engine running. Jerry came out a few seconds later hefting a large carpetbag, jumped in the car and told me to move.

Al had been shot, Jerry told me as I drove back to the Bronx. We both hoped that he'd been killed. If not he would talk, and then be double-tapped and probably thrown in the East River with a block of cement chained to his ankles.

Jerry took Al's share of the money, and I ended up with a third, which was over forty thousand bucks.

It was the day after the robbery that Jerry got the call from Al's cell. A guy told him that Al had lived long enough to spill his guts in more ways than one. Gave Jerry an ultimatum; return every penny and live, or be stupid and wind up like Al.

I was all for giving the money back, but Jerry said it most likely belonged to the mob, and that we would be whacked whichever way we played it.

I decided to run. I gave Angie ten grand and told her to pack a case and walk away from the apartment; that her life was at risk. And then I just hit the road and kept moving. But my face was out there. I grew a beard, had my long hair cut short, and just lived on hope and paid my way with the stolen money, staying at fleapit motels and using different names in every town I stayed at. I didn't know it, but my luck was running out like gas in the leaking tank of a fast moving car.

I ordered another large shot of bourbon and waited. I'd called in at the Wolf Trap Bar for a drink, and to decide on where to head for the next morning. But this was surely going to be my final destination. The wall-mounted phone had rung, and the bartender had answered it, listened, and then looked at me and said that if I was Johnny Porter, then it was for me.

I don't know who it was that I talked to. I didn't ask because it didn't matter. He said that Jerry was dead, and that they'd traced Angie, and that if I didn't want her to be fed into an industrial meat grinder, then I should just stay exactly where I was and not to do anything stupid when someone approached me.

Another drink dulled my fear a little more. When the small guy wearing a pork pie hat – like the one that Hackman had worn in *The French connection* – walked in the door and made a beeline for me, I even smiled.

He told me to leave the bar by the back door and get in the rear of a black SUV with tinted windows.

He took the empty gun from my holster as we walked out into the dark lot.

I asked him how they had found me. He said that they had eyes everywhere, and that Angie had given them photos of me. He wanted what was left of the money, and I told him it was in a rucksack, back at the motel I was staying at, hidden in the roof space.

Funny, but as my personal sands of time were running out I felt a certain amount of relief. I had no hope left and living had lost most of its appeal. I got in the back of the car and

Pork Pie sat beside me, pressing the muzzle of a pistol into my ribs. He told the guy at the wheel to drive to my motel.

There was no moon, and the country road was narrow. Coincidence struck again. A big truck came round a tight curve on the wrong side, heading straight for us. Both vehicles swerved, but still collided, fender to fender. The truck turned over and its load of potatoes rained down on the 4x4, which had come to a stop sideways on to it.

The driver had not buckled up, and had shot through the windshield like a human cannonball, to hit a tree with enough force to break his skull apart like an egg being cracked on the edge of a skillet.

Pork Pie was moaning. There was a ribbon of blood flowing from his mouth, and he was hugging his chest. I saw his gun in the foot well, so picked it up.

I asked him where Angie was, and he told me not to be stupid: that they had all had a piece of her, and then got rid of the body, permanently.

It only took me a minute to inflict enough pain on the hoodlum to be told the name of his boss; the man who'd ordered that Angie be raped and murdered. I took Pork Pie's wallet and cell phone from him, and then pushed the barrel of the gun into his stomach, angled it down and pulled the trigger, twice.

I got out and also took the phone and wallet from the corpse of the driver, and then found the teamster. He was also beyond help. When someone came across the two vehicles and the three bodies it would look like what it had been, an RTA. It would be a while before the police or paramedics discovered that one of the corpses had two bullets in his gut.

With what Pork Pie had told me, and the contact lists in the phones, I had all the information I needed. I collected the rucksack from the motel, hotwired an old Chevy from a side street in town and headed east. There was no hurry. After driving for a hundred miles I stopped in another small town, changed plates with a Pontiac and kept moving. I felt a flood of emotions. I wanted to live now; to avenge Angie by taking out all those that had been involved in what had happened to her.

Rage and then purpose had combined to bring about a change in my outlook. I had an agenda, and that was basically what all people needed: a reason to live.

HAVE A GOOD LIFE

I took another sip of the now lukewarm black coffee and thought about the people I intended to kill as I used a paper serviette to clear a circular patch in the condensation that filmed the plate glass window. It was four o'clock in the morning, and dawn was already breaking, lightening the eastern horizon as it heralded another new day.

I was in limbo both physically and mentally, between two places in mind and body at this service area on the MI.

Maybe I was getting too old for the game. I felt bone-tired, my right knee was swollen with arthritis that caused me to limp, and without spectacles with Coke bottle-thick lenses I would have needed a guide dog and a white stick. The urge to quit and move to warmer climes grew stronger every day. And I had enough money tucked away to buy a decent place in Spain, or anywhere that offered more warmth than the UK throughout the year. Greed was not the issue. I was a pro, and the service I provided was second to none. I could truthfully say, like Tina Turner sang, that I was 'Simply the Best'.

I flexed my leg a few times, popped a couple of anti-inflammatory caps and washed them down with the gritty dregs of the coffee, then went into the gents to take a piss and rinse my face. As I patted it dry I caught a look at my reflection in the mirror above the sink. God! I looked more like my late father every day. I was only forty-eight, but could have been taken for a sodding pensioner.

Just this one last gig up in Leeds, I decided, then back down to London, collect the balance of my payment for the double-header hit, and bow out.

Bands of low-lying morning fog striped the motorway, swirling like rafts of cigarette smoke as I squinted through the windscreen and eased back to little more than thirty miles an hour. I went through the plan again; of the crime I would soon commit. It would be a doddle. John Carson and his wife, Pamela, had both worked as research chemists for Zygol Laboratories, and had stolen a formula that any of a dozen competitors in the field would give an arm and a leg for. My contract was not to simply eliminate the couple, but to first retrieve a coded flash drive in their possession. They were renting a riverside apartment under assumed names, and currently conducting an international auction over the net, with every intention of selling the stolen information to the highest bidder. I slipped photographs of the couple out of the manila folder on the passenger seat. They were both in their late thirties, looked to be intelligent, but obviously lacked commonsense. They should have known that you don't commit industrial espionage on this scale without putting your life on the line.

I couldn't foresee any complications. Hopefully they would give up the USB without me having to resort to using unnecessary violence. I prided myself on being the consummate professional; a specialist if you will, who executed quick, clean kills. I wasn't one of those psychos that wanted to control, dominate and float my boat by meting out protracted torture. It was business, pure and simple. I was a hitman who completed my contracts with as little fuss as possible. It was never personal. Marks were just strangers. And If I didn't take on the job of dealing with them, then someone else would.

Damn it! The fog and traffic were conspiring against me. I was running late. I should have driven up North the day before and stayed over, but I liked to get in and out quick, to be seen by as few people as possible.

Finally arriving in the area in which the couple lived, I parked the Cherokee a couple of streets away and walked in. I wore shades, and a baseball cap with its bill pulled down. I didn't look up. I'd noticed the CCTV camera covering the entrance door, but my features were obscured. I pressed one of the buttons on the panel at random with the knuckle of my index finger and waited. The intercom crackled.

"Yeah?"

It was a man's voice. Good. As a rule they weren't as suspicious and twitchy as women.

"Electricity Board," I said, affecting a Welsh accent to obscure my London twang. "I need to get in and check out the main fuse box."

"Are you going to cut us off?"

"Not if I can help it, sir."

There was a buzz and the lock disengaged.

I took the stairs up to the third floor, ignoring the fire in my knee. Before exiting the stairwell I pulled a pair of kidskin gloves on, and then screwed the silencer onto the muzzle of my 9 millimeter Browning pistol. I was ready to rock 'n' roll, with adrenaline pumping me up in anticipation of completing my task.

There was no answer to the door. They were out. I shoved the gun into the waistband of my chinos, quickly withdrew a leather wallet containing lock picks, and was inside the apartment within thirty seconds. All I could do now was wait it out. I was dealing with a naive pair of Muppets. They'd seen an opportunity to get rich quick and gone for it, without considering how dire the consequences of their actions might be.

Settling down in the lounge with a bottle of Scotch purloined from a wall unit in the kitchen, I poured myself a generous measure and tried to relax. I felt unsettled. All of a sudden my heart wasn't in it. The older I got, the more I appreciated life, which was a fleeting gift, to be cherished and not taken lightly or for granted. And yet I had made a very lucrative livelihood out of abruptly ending that which I was now beginning to hold sacred. Don't get me wrong, my conscience wasn't pricking me for past sins I'd committed. Some of the marks I'd hit deserved all they got, to my way of thinking. But I felt that I had reached a saturation point. Was a spark of moral decency rearing its ugly head? It didn't do for a stone killer to examine the right and wrong of his actions. I was a hired gun, not a philosopher or a contender for the Nobel peace prize. I had long ago rationalised that many people perish needlessly every day by way of disease, accident, famine, war, and even by their own hand. Surely my hastening the demise of a few less than pure pilgrims was of little consequence in the greater scheme of things. Mine was not to reason why, but to make damn sure the chosen die.

I was losing my touch. I actually fell asleep. On waking, my heart thundered in my chest like a caged animal hurling itself against the bars in an effort to escape. For a moment I had no idea of where I was. On hearing muffled voices out in the corridor I picked up the glass and half empty Scotch bottle and only just made it into the master bedroom before someone entered the apartment.

From within the floor-to-ceiling wardrobe that ran the length of one wall, I listened to the conversation between John and Pamela Carson:

"Can you believe it, Pam? Three million pounds for a poxy flash drive. By tomorrow afternoon the deal will be done and the money will be transferred to a bank account in the Cayman Islands."

"I'm scared, John. What if something—"

"Don't worry, love, nothing can go wrong. Nobody knows where we are, and as soon as we hand this over we can catch the first plane out. Let's open a bottle of wine and celebrate."

I hunkered down in the darkness and nursed the pistol as the couple clinked glasses together and began to giggle. They thought that all their Christmases had come at once, and that they were just a few hours' away from embarking on a new life; rich beyond their wildest dreams.

How blessed we are, *not* to be able to see what lies ahead. It might be advantageous to dip into the near future and glean information regarding stock market prices, race results, or of course the winning Lotto numbers. But there's always a downside. Who would want to have foreknowledge of death and disaster: To know that a 747 was going to drop from the sky and plough into a housing estate, or that an earthquake would wipe out a city and cause incalculable loss of life? And who would believe it if you tried to warn them? No thank you. One day at a time, sweet Jesus, as some old gospel song goes. Ignorance can be bliss, and preserve sanity in a mad, mad world.

It was half an hour later that they came through to the bedroom. By then my bad knee was locked-up, and in the stifling confines of the wardrobe my clothes were sticking to me with sweat. It was like being in a sauna with the light off. I could have stepped out at any time and confronted them, but for some reason let them enjoy the moment. Was I going soft?

They both froze, mouths hanging open as I emerged and levelled the gun at the man's chest.

"I want the USB, now," I said to him. "Do you understand? No stalling, talking or pleading ignorance. Just get it."

My voice broke the spell and the woman spoke.

"Are...are you going to kill us?" Pamela said.

"You know I am, sweetheart," I said. "You went for broke, and lost."

"Please, *don't* do it," she implored. "Just take the stick. You don't have to...to shoot us. We're no threat to anyone."

"It's not that simple," I replied, as if I needed to justify what I was about to do. "I have a contract to fulfil."

With the stick safely in my pocket I ordered them both to sit on the edge of the bed with their backs to me, and then I pushed the cold steel of the silencer up against Pamela Carson's head. She began to sob as my finger tightened on the trigger.

A week later I was sitting in the shade under a palm tree, sipping a chilled beer. The bar was directly opposite the bank, and I was in no particular hurry. George Town on Grand

Cayman was colourful, busy, and a perfect location to start my retirement.

John came out of the bank and walked across the street to where Pamela and I waited.

"There," he said, handing me a bankers' cheque for a million and a half dollars.

I smiled at each of them in turn. "Thanks," I said. "I can honestly say that it has been a pleasure doing business with you. Have a good life."

THE BEST LAID PLANS

INITIALLY it was just a small and uncultivated idea that grew and began to possess her. And then like a fertile seed it germinated in her mind, put down roots in her brain and evolved with time.

Marion Wrigglesworth made the decision to murder her husband. It was only the how, where and when to do it that had to be worked out. She had no intention of rushing into it, to be subsequently caught and spend many years in prison. Anything worth doing was worth doing well, and Marion was nothing if not meticulous in all her endeavours.

The marriage had proved to be lacklustre over time, but neither of them had entered into it with great expectation, and would in hindsight have been better friends than partners; a mutual love of book reading and rambling in the countryside not being strong enough to sustain the relationship. They had both worked at the local library, where Marion was still a clerk, and Brian had been the Chief Librarian. The bond between them had grown when they found themselves alone one evening after closing and had engaged in a spontaneous bout of love – or was it lust – making on the hardwood floor, between the towering rows of true crime and biographies. The following year they had married at the local registry office, spent a rainy honeymoon in a caravan at Bridlington on the east coast, and on their return to Leeds moved in with Brian's elderly mother, in the semidetached house that he had been born and raised in.

Perhaps it was the twenty-four-year age difference between them that shaped the way they were. Marion was now forty-one, and Brian, sixty-five; a certified bus pass-carrying pensioner who was suffering a multitude of ailments, was old at heart, content to sit in front of the television these days, and invariably went to bed before ten p.m.

Marion had come to despise him. Since his mother had died eight years ago Brian had become ill-tempered and morose, no longer the pleasant and mild-mannered man that she had known. She felt more like a carer than a wife. It wasn't fair. She wasn't living, just existing within a loveless and empty marriage. She wanted a little pleasure out of life; to go to concerts, out for meals, maybe dancing, and to fulfil a dream by going on a cruise in the Med and perhaps having an onboard fling. You only lived once, and she was now begrudging every day that passed. Brian had to go, it was as simple as that.

Of course she could have just walked out and left him. But she had no intention of ending up with next to nothing, after putting up with him for so long. She'd given him the best years of her life, and was determined to see something for it. The house was worth at least two hundred and fifty thousand pounds, and she knew that Brian had insurance, and a building society account that he thought she didn't know about. Having said that, she had also been squirreling a little money away for herself over the years. All in all with him out of the way she would be comfortably off, and have the means and freedom to spread her wings and make up for what now seemed like lost time.

"Marion," Brian called from the lounge. "It's nine-thirty. I'm thirsty."

She took deep breaths. Clenched her fists and counted to ten. This was definitely the last time she would make him a cup of cocoa before he shuffled up to bed, to climb into it wearing the grimy boxer shorts and socks that he had not changed for at least a week. God! He was disgusting.

"Drink it while it's hot, dear," she said, placing the steaming mug on the nest of tables next to the recliner chair on which he was stretched out reading a Wilbur Smith paperback.

"What have you been doing, Marion?" he asked, voice mushy without the benefit of his ill-fitting National Health dentures. "You've been in the kitchen all evening."

"Just sorting through the home file," she lied. "It needed clearing out. There were stacks of old paid bills and stuff."

Brian hiked his bony shoulders with indifference and slurped noisily at the cocoa, sucking off the skin that had formed on its surface. She would've liked to have put rat poison in it, but that was a no-no. Her choice of doing away with him was severely limited. She watched shows like CSI: Crime Scene Investigation, and knew all about retrieval of trace evidence. Forensic science made murder a risky undertaking. She had considered a score of ways to do the deed, and had narrowed the list down to just two. He was going to die by either electric shock or the trauma of being pushed down the stairs. And explaining an electrical appliance ending up in the bath might prove difficult and arouse suspicion. A swift push in the back as he was about to come down the stairs was favourite. The more simple the better. His ailing heart would be her ally. He had suffered two minor cardiac infarctions in less than three years and was on beta-blockers. But what if he just fractured a few bones and survived, despite his frailty, to accuse her? Nothing was certain. But she was now fresh out of patience and wanted it to be over with. If he didn't do them both a favour and break his fucking scrawny neck or have a massive heart attack when he fell, then she would have to finish him off; the way you'd put an injured animal out of its misery. She would loosen one of the old wooden uprights in the banister, and if necessary pull it free and administer the coup de grâce, wearing a heavy-duty Marigold glove to wield it. There would be no fingerprints, and she would damage the banister further. It would be plausible that he had gone through it as he fell. And maybe he would. Once sure that he was beyond help, she would phone for an ambulance, act suitably hysterical, but not overdo it, and wait a respectable length of time before changing her lifestyle, quitting her job at the library and picking up brochures from the travel agent.

Marion hardly slept, not because of Brian's loud snoring from the other single bed, but due to the excitement and anticipation of being free from what had become an unbearable encumbrance.

Up at six a.m., Marion brewed tea and took her cup out into the small back garden, to sit in her robe and slippers at the rustic table on the patio and listen to the birds singing. It was going to be a glorious June day, and not wholly due to the weather. She had decided to murder Brian that evening, after they had eaten. At some point he would go upstairs to the loo, and she would be waiting for him when he came out.

A pigeon flapped noisily overhead and deposited a large white dropping that spattered on the timber tabletop less than an inch from her cup. Was that a portent of good or bad luck? Maybe neither. It was just what it was; bird shit.

After showering and dressing, Marion took a cup of tea up to Brian, who was still in bed, and forced herself to give him a fleeting peck on the forehead before going back downstairs and leaving the house, to walk along George Street and through the market place, stopping outside Far & Wide Travel to gaze at the posters in the window. One showed a large cruise liner. It was majestic, a dazzling white, and was moored off a tropical shore next to a palm tree fringed a sugary beach. Now that was a good omen. In a month or two she would be on the balcony of a first class cabin with a glass of champagne in hand.

It was hard to concentrate on work that day. She was daydreaming and planning to go on a diet and shed a couple of stones, buy new clothes, and send off for a passport. The Mediterranean was now dismissed. She had decide to go the whole hog and cruise the Caribbean, calling in at places like Grand Cayman and the Bahamas, to maybe swim with dolphins. She felt truly alive for the first time in her life. All the things that she had never done were waiting, just around the corner, only separated from her by an old man who took no pleasure from life, and whose death would be a rebirth for her.

He was asleep in front of the TV when she arrived home. She didn't wake him, just went upstairs to have another shower and get changed, before making the tea. He would have a last meal befitting a condemned man; steak with all the trimmings, followed by apple pie and custard for dessert; his favourite.

"That smells good," he called. "What are we having, love."

"Fillet steak," she replied. "You'd better put your teeth in."

After they'd eaten, Marion had second thoughts. The magnitude of what she intended to do was making her light-headed. Her whole body was shaking. Would she, could she go through with it? She wasn't without emotion. The burden of guilt might sour any pleasure she contemplated.

"That was wonderful, dear," Brian said, sitting back and belching loudly.

He had the manners of a pig. It was that one long, rolling belch that strengthened her resolve. He was going to die.

It was eight o'clock and still broad daylight outside when Brian pushed himself up groaning with the effort, and shambled out into the hall oohing and aahing against his multiple aches and pains as he slowly climbed the stairs.

Now or never, Marion thought. She waited until the bathroom door squeaked shut and then tiptoed up to the landing, went into the nearest bedroom and hid behind the door.

Jesus wept! Had he died in there? That would save her the job. It was the longest fifteen minutes of her life. A small eternity. Beads of sweat pricked her scalp, ran out from her mousy hair and formed rivulets that streamed down her forehead and into her eyes, making them sting as she blinked rapidly to expel them. Her chubby hands were clammy and palsied.

At last, the toilet flushed and Brian came out of the bathroom and walked over to the top of the stairs. He made to descend them, but caught a blur of movement from the corner of his eye as Marion rushed forward with her arms outstretched as she emitted a wavering high-pitched cry. Her small, porcine eyes were wide open; a wild and almost insane look in them.

It was without doubt the fastest that Marion had ever seen Brian move. Even as the palms of her hands were within a hairsbreadth of making contact with his stooped back, he jerked sideways against the wall.

It didn't make sense. His brain couldn't fathom out what had gotten into Marion. She sailed out into the air, a piercing scream hurting his ears as she performed an ungainly dive without having the benefit of water to land in. The scream was abruptly curtailed as her head hit a stair halfway down. And the subsequent loud crack was almost certainly her neck breaking like a twig.

Brian watched horror-stricken as Marion came to rest in a very unnatural pose on the carpet in the hallway. Her eyes were staring up at him, but unseeing, and her frozen expression was one of total surprise.

It was almost impossible for Brian to entertain the belief that his wife had intended to murder him, but there seemed no other explanation. He phoned the emergency services and told them that his wife had fallen down the stairs, and that he believed she was dead. He was numb with shock and deeply saddened. He had always relied on her, perhaps taken her for granted, and was now suddenly alone and afraid of how he might cope with her no longer there to look after him.

A VISIT FROM JIMMY THE FISH

TOMMY Pierce was sitting in an old leather easy chair in the small living room of the terrace house on Willis Street in Hackney, which had belonged to his late parents. He was wearing a grubby grey T-shirt and almost matching piss-stained boxer shorts. The TV was on, quite loud because he was partially deaf, due to having played heavy metal music full blast for several years. The final session of the Masters' snooker from Ally Pally was on the box, but he was not watching it; just shaking like a leaf in a strong breeze as he looked across to the two-seater settee where Jimmy 'The Fish' Skirrow was sitting and staring at him with big, watery cod eyes that gave no insight as to his emotions. Tommy had thought that the knock at the door was Ray Harper calling round with a bottle of Scotch and a take-away meal, to celebrate the heist, but it had been Skirrow with a gun in his hand.

Jimmy kept the silenced 9mm Glock pointing rock solid at Tommy's chest and said, "You're a wanker, Tommy. Coming south of the river with that meth head Harper and ripping off a poker game that Vic Jennings had arranged was definitely the dumbest freakin' thing you've ever done. Did you really think that you could get away with it?"

"We…we didn't know that Vic was running it," Tommy said. "And we had ski masks on, so how—?"

"How did we know it was you two losers?" Jimmy said, showing off his tea-stain-coloured teeth as he gave Tommy a lopsided grin. "Because Harper always wears a big silver skull pinkie ring, and being a complete amateur he left it on when you both barged in with sawn-off shotguns, stole sixty grand and ruined the boss's evening."

"I can make it right," Tommy said.

"That's a given. Same as Harper did. He gave his half of the money back and grassed you up as being his accomplice."

"The money is in a carrier bag in the kitchen, in the sink unit behind a pile of cleaning stuff. It's all there."

"So lead the way and get it."

Tommy retrieved the bag, and Jimmy told him to empty it out on the kitchen table, count it in front oh him, stack it in five grand piles and then put it in the large briefcase that he had brought with him and placed on the table with the lid open.

"So far, so good," Jimmy said, once it was done. "Now sit on a chair and pull the bag over your head."

"Please, no, you don't have to do this," Tommy said. "Don't shoot me."

"Just following orders," Jimmy said. "The boss wants an example made, to let other punks know that stepping over the line comes with a high price tag."

Tommy wanted to make a play, but Jimmy was standing too far away from him. There was no way that he would be able to reach the guy without taking a bullet.

"The bag," Jimmy said. "Do it now."

Tommy slowly pulled the plastic carrier bag over his head and sat down on a rail back chair and clenched his hands on its arms in a white-knuckle grip. He had never been so terrified in his life. This was it. Jesus! He was going to be shot to death. Sweat bubbled out of his scalp and forehead as he sucked in the scant amount of air trapped in the bag. He could hear himself making a whining sound as he screwed his eyelids tightly shut, gritted his teeth and waited for whatever it felt like to have a bullet drill through his brain.

After letting him suffer whatever feelings someone facing death must undergo for at least twenty seconds, Jimmy pulled the trigger.

Tommy cried out in agony and fell forward, to topple out of the chair. The bullet had gone through the back of his right hand, to pass through the pine wood and blast a hole in the linoleum before ricocheting off the underlying concrete and embed in the wall near the kitchen door.

"It's your lucky day," Jimmy said. "The boss said that as long as he got the money back, to just give you a strong incentive not to come over to our side of the river again with bad intentions."

Job done. Jimmy left the house. He was on his own time now and had arranged to meet his bird, Jacquie, for an evening meal at a curry house in Bermondsey.

Tommy ripped the bag off his head and stared at the penny-sized entry hole in the back of his hand. There was massive hole in the palm, a lot of blood pooling on the floor, and he was in agony, but relieved to still be alive. He guessed that Ray had got the same treatment, and had been warned off from giving him a bell and telling him that Vic Jennings had sent an enforcer to recover the money and mete out punishment.

MY NAME IS BENNY TAYLOR

BEING dyslexic was just one of Benny Taylor's several problems. Although he did not even know that the condition existed. Being partially word blind was just something he had grown up with. Had he attended school more often, then it might have been picked up on, but truancy was his chosen way of spending his days. The video game arcade was a far more enjoyable place to be than school. Hanging out with like-minded mates was preferable to sitting in a classroom, bored stiff and unable to take anything in, and not giving a shit what date the Battle of bloody Hastings had gone down. Here and now was all that mattered to him.

Benny was street-wise; a seasoned criminal at fifteen years old, who was a dab hand at picking pockets, shoplifting, and even burglary. There was no one or nothing to stop him being a law unto himself. His father, Ronnie, was serving ten years for his part as the getaway driver in a failed bank robbery. And his mother, Gail, worked at a laundry six days a week, and then went out every evening to drown her sorrows and play the field, making hay while the sun shone, as she put it, while Ronnie was safely tucked up in Strangeways nick.

It was an old movie that gave Benny the idea to set his sights much higher. In the film, a young guy was robbing post offices, getting away with lots of money, and living the high life. You didn't need an education to get rich quick, just a sawn-off shotgun and enough bottle to go for it. And what did it matter if he got caught? He had done a stretch in borstal and it was no big deal. Most of the time inside he'd played snooker, smoked joints and watched TV. True, he'd been made to work on the nick's pig farm, and that had been the scariest thing he'd ever done. Some of those old porkers were as big as rhinos, farted a lot, and had a seriously bad attitude. Being turned into rashers of bacon was all they were good for.

Stealing a BMX from outside the Co-op, Benny rode out to see Vinny; a man who worked at the local landfill site. Vinny could get anything for anyone, at a price.

"Whadya need a shotgun for, Benny?" Vinny said as he aimed an air rifle at one of the numerous rats that had made the site their home. "You gonna try an' rob a bank an' be like your old man?"

"No. I thought I'd blag a post office."

Vinny took a deep breath, let it out slowly and eased his finger back smoothly on the trigger. A rat that was gnawing through a bulging black bin bag leapt into the air, twisting and screaming as the lead pellet thudded into its side. It crawled off into the mountains of rubbish as Vinny chuckled and reloaded, before turning to Benny and saying, "Bad idea, son, you'll end up doin' serious bird. Why not stick to small stuff?"

"Because I need serious money. I'm goin' to set up in business."

"Doin' what?"

"I'm not sure, yet. Maybe buyin' discontinued clothin' and stuff from catalogues. I could open a shop, or get a market stall."

"Dream on, son. You wouldn't like workin' for a livin'."

"You work, Vinny."

"Nah. I just open up, tell drivers were to dump their loads, and..." he fired at another rat, missed it and cursed. "...see how many rats I can blow away. The pay's not much, but I have an easy life."

"Sweet," Benny said. "Will you get hold of a shotgun for me, eh?"

"Yeah, but it'll cost you."

Planning and preparation was the key to success. Benny was badly educated but not stupid. He knew that there would be CCTV cameras, and that the idiots behind the counter probably had alarm buttons that they could operate with their feet if need be. He was no mug. He would wear sunglasses, a baseball cap, and keep his head down. And the old 12 bore that Vinny had got him was now short enough to push into the waistband of his cargo pants. He'd used a hacksaw to take eighteen inches off the barrels.

Vinny had even thrown in a dozen cartridges. Benny thought it through. He had no intention of shooting anyone. He didn't want to end up doing life. But he might need to blast a hole in the ceiling to show them that he meant business.

The last part was the hardest. He had to have a note to hand to whoever was behind the counter. It would have to be taken seriously, and the fact that he couldn't read or write was a major problem.

He went back to see Vinny.

"Sixteen! I've sent sixteen of the humpbacked, disease-ridden fur balls to rat heaven this mornin', Benny," Vinny said. "That's my all-time record so far."

"Nice one, Vinny. You're the 'Exterminator' like Arnie Scwartzwhatever. You should get paid extra for pest control."

"Arnie was the Terminator, you idiot."

"Whatever. I need for you to do me a favour."

"What kind of favour?"

"Just a note to hand to the bird behind the counter."

Vinny's office was a small brick-built building. Just one room, or two if you counted the toilet at the rear. But he had made the place a home. He was supposed to lock up and leave the premises each evening, but actually stayed over a lot, sleeping on a settee that he had reclaimed from one of the skips. Being superintendent of the tip was not just a job to him. He loved what he did, liked his own company, and was now totally addicted to shooting rats. It was war.

"Whadya want me to write?" Vinny said, holding a biro poised over a sheet of coffee-stained notepaper.

"How about: 'Put all the money in the bag. And don't try anythin' stupid or I'll blow your fuckin' head off'. Somethin' like that."

Vinny scribbled, folded the piece of paper in half and slipped it into an envelope.

"There you go, Benny. And be careful, son, because these people are as nervous as rats, they expect to be robbed."

Benny had planned to do the job the next day, but his mum foiled that by getting beaten up in the high-rise's lift. She said that the guy who had walked her home from the pub had got a little frisky, then violent when she told him to sod off.

Benny had called an ambulance. Gail had a fractured cheek, a broken rib puncturing her left lung, and both front teeth missing. Her face had swollen up like a balloon, and she was kept in the Royal.

"Who was it, Mum?" Benny asked her as she lay moaning in the hospital bed.

"I don't know, love. I'd never seen him before last night. Forget about it. He isn't worth gettin' into trouble over."

Gail did not want Benny on the guy's case. Trouble with her son was, he had a psychotic temper; had always been a problem child, and although a little calmer at fifteen, was almost six foot tall and built like a prop forward. The lad didn't know his own strength. Gail had not forgotten the council official who had been giving her grief over outstanding rent. Benny had hung him over the railings of the walkway by his ankles, and the man had screamed like a baby as he looked down at the roof of a torched car twelve floors below him.

"You want for me to drop him, Mum?" Benny had asked her.

"Better not, son," she had replied. "I think he's got the message."

They lived in a rough area. It was a human jungle with danger at every turn.

Ten days passed, and life went back to whatever passed for normal. Gail returned to work at the laundry, still hurting but needing the money. And Benny made ready to commit his first armed post office robbery. He had a lot more sense than his dad. No partners in crime to grass him up to the Bill. He determined to always work alone, and not get *too* greedy.

It was a cold and dismal autumn day when he walked into the post office. There were two queues, mostly made up of wrinklies buying TV stamps, paying bills and posting stuff. He was in no hurry. He held the envelope in his hand, remembered to keep his face angled down towards the floor, and just waited his turn.

Karen Connelly finally got rid of Edna Pearson; a widow who came in for a chat as much as to pick up her benefits. Funny how old people acted as though they had all the time in the world, when in truth many of them were past their sell-by date and hadn't got a lot of time left to them.

Karen could see her reflection in the mirrored shades that the young man now facing her was wearing. Why wear sunglasses on a grey October day? Everything about him caused her to be glad that she was separated from customers by bullet-proof glass. He had a fixed smile on his face that made her shiver. And he didn't say a word, just pushed a dog-eared envelope through the slot in front of her.

"Can you see to that for me, please?" Benny said.

Karen pulled out the sheet of paper and opened it. There were brown blotches on it that looked like coffee. And the writing was a spidery scrawl. She read it, frowned, and then ducked down as she saw the youth produce what she recognised as being a sawn-off shotgun.

"I've pressed the alarm," Karen shouted up to him from where she was crouching out of sight. "The police will be here in less than a minute."

Benny panicked, aimed the shotgun at the ceiling and pulled the trigger. There was just a loud click. He turned and ran, sending an old man sprawling as he bolted out of the door and legged it down the street.

Back home, after dumping the weapon in the nearby canal, Benny decided that he would stick to small stuff.

Ten minutes later there was a knock at the door. His mum would have forgotten her key again. When he opened it, he was rushed by armed police, who quickly wrestled him to the floor and handcuffed him. *How had they known who he was?*

Vinny was sitting in his office eating a cheese and onion sandwich when the news of the failed robbery and subsequent capture of the teenage offender was reported on a radio that he had salvaged, cleaned up and put fresh batteries in. He shook his head. Benny was not safe to be on the street. He had done him a favour. A year or two inside would do him no harm at all. If the lad could read or write, then he might still be free as a bird. But Vinny had not written what Benny had dictated. Instead he had written: My name is Benny Taylor, and I live in flat 126 at Holbeck Tower. The cartridges in the gun I have are duds. Call the police.

It didn't do to have idiots like Benny on the loose; Vinny thought as he finished his sandwich, wiped crumbs from his grizzled chin with the back of his hand, picked up his air rifle and went back outside to lay in wait for his furry prey.

A NOT SO PURRFECT MURDER

IF anyone ever tells you that it's easy to kill another human being, *do not* believe them for a second, unless you know for a fact that they are practising homicidal psychopaths.

Reg Barker was now a killer and felt sick to the stomach as he stood in the dimly lit confines of his garage, trembling and shocked, his clothing soaked with blood as he surveyed the still, crumpled figure of his next-door neighbour, Albert Sewell, sprawled out on a large piece of tarpaulin.

It had been an accident. Really. But it would be hard to prove that and, at sixty-five years old, Reg was not going to take the risk of being arrested and tried for murder. Spending the remaining years of his life behind bars was not on his list of 'things to do'.

The engine of the chainsaw idled as Reg pondered several irrational solutions to cover up his actions. He wasn't thinking rationally as he pulled the trigger back, to hunker down and begin to dismember the man who had for many years been his closest friend.

The sudden and total breakdown of their long-term relationship had been the result of an affair that Reg had begun with Albert's wife, Doreen. Or to be more precise, due to him allowing Doreen to seduce him. Albert's work had necessitated his being over in Liverpool for three days a week. And while the cat was away, his buxom blonde mouse wanted to play.

Reg fervently wished that he'd had the resolve to turn her down. But it was hard to spurn the advances of a more than reasonably attractive woman with curves in all the right places and the added bonus of her being more than a decade his junior.

He took a break, gasping for breath with the effort of sawing through muscle and bone with a heavy chainsaw that was in dire need of having its blunt teeth sharpened. Albert always had been a tough old boot. Christ, Reg thought, how could it have come to this? As if he didn't know.

Letting the past drift back in, – like morning fog in the dale beyond the two isolated semidetached cottages that stood in whitewashed splendour on the quiet B road – Reg vividly recalled the day that Doreen had left Albert for Neil Jennings, a local parish councillor.

Albert had hammered on his door that night, cursing and threatening to kill him. "Call yourself a friend?" Albert had said. "Don't think I don't know what you and Doreen got up to. She told me everything before she took off with Jennings. If I owned a bloody shotgun, I swear I'd blow your head off."

"I don't know what she told you, Albert, but it's a lie," Reg said. But he could hear the hollow echo of deceit in his own voice. And that was that. They hadn't spoken a word to each other from that day forth. Not until this grey and blustery October morning.

Reg had been sawing off some wrist-thick branches that were hanging over the boundary fence between their back gardens. He'd cut them well back, even stretching to saw them on Albert's side.

Albert had rushed out, to limp across the lawn brandishing his walking cane, ignoring the fact that he was in dire need of a hip replacement as he vented his rage.

"You're trespassing with that infernal machine," Albert shouted, to be heard above the loud sound of the petrol-powered chainsaw. "Stop chopping my trees down, or I'll…I'll…"

Reg took his finger off the trigger and said, "You'll what?" as he smirked at Albert.

"You'll be sorry, you old goat," Albert said, giving him a look that could have thawed ice on the village pond.

"Is that a threat?" Reg demanded.

"No, it's a promise," Albert said, reaching up, taking a swing with his horn-handled hickory cane and cracking Reg across the knuckles.

Reg yelped at the sudden pain and almost fell off the ladder. "You've gone too far, Sewell, you maniac," he seethed through clenched teeth, and promptly reached over as far as he could and triggered the saw to slice the top three feet off a fir tree that he knew Albert had planted over a decade before, and that he prized.

"That does it," Albert screamed, and ran to the front of his cottage; rage dulling the fiery pain in his hip.

Reg knew that there was going to be a confrontation that could result in a nasty altercation, and was not prepared to end up rolling around on the damp grass exchanging punches. Albert had a mean temper, and had been a fair boxer back in his army days.

Albert marched across Reg's lawn, and they faced each other like two ageing gunfighters on the dusty street of some Wild West town.

Albert had had time to reflect on what might transpire as he made his way to the front of his neighbour's cottage. Reg was over six feet tall, outweighed him by at least three stone, and had once pinned a door-to-door salesman up against his garage wall with his feet off the ground, because the pushy guy wouldn't take no for an answer.

But Albert was too proud to lose face. "Apologise for what you just did, and we'll say no more about it," he said

"Apologise to you? You must be joking," Reg growled as he pulled the cord to restart the saw. "You could have broken my fingers, you stupid geriatric fart. Get the hell off my property, before I throw you off."

Albert saw red and charged at Reg, lashing out with his cane.

It all happened in the space between two seconds. Reg swung the chainsaw up defensively and the metal teeth cut through the improvised weapon as if it was butter, to then make contact with the side of Albert's neck.

Reg had never seen so much blood in his life. Albert shrieked, clasped his hands to the gaping rent and spun around in what resembled a macabre dance, before keeling over and laying on his back, his mouth opening and closing like that of a goldfish out of water.

It was over very quickly. Albert bled out and became still, and his sightless eyes stared heavenward with an expression of total shock frozen in them.

After backing his car out, Reg dragged the body in through the side door of the garage and wished he could turn back the clock ten minutes and undo what had happened. But wishes were just so much straw in the wind. You had to deal with what is, not what might, could, or should have been.

"Get away. Shoo," Reg said to Claws, an old Tomcat that his late wife had taken in when it was a kitten, fifteen years ago. The cat was hunched up next to Albert's head, lapping at the spreading pool of blood on the concrete floor. It ignored Reg, until he lashed out with his foot, to send it scurrying off, hissing like a snake.

And now, after bagging up the multiple pieces of Albert in black plastic bin liners, Reg went into the cottage and poured a large and much needed Scotch, to drink it neat in two swallows. He coughed as the alcohol burned its way down into his stomach, but it settled his nerves a little, and so he had another one and began to feel much better.

A cold, dispassionate mood pervaded him. He knew what he had to do: dispose of the body parts in a place where they would not be discovered, and meticulously clean up all traces of Albert having ever been on his property. All the CSI-type TV shows made it clear that it was forensic science that led to the apprehension of many criminals.

Two days passed. Albert's body parts were now safely entombed in a deep, disused well fifteen miles away, and the garage floor and walls had been scrubbed three times with piping hot water containing strong bleach. Reg had also been round the garden, hosing away blood that had sprayed onto the grass.

No worries. Funny, but he didn't even feel guilty. Albert had started it, and paid the price. And maybe, subconsciously, he had meant to cut his neighbour's throat with the chainsaw. Whatever. He had no motive and was convinced that he would never be suspected of foul play.

It was several days later that two plainclothes policemen came to his door.

"What can I do for you?" Reg said to the officers, manufacturing a frown as he was shown their warrant cards.

"It's about your next door neighbour, sir," DC Terry Nelhams said. "It appears he's gone missing; just dropped below the radar, so to speak. We wondered if you might have any idea where he might have gone."

"Sorry," Reg said. "Old Albert was a bit of a recluse. We didn't even speak to each other. He kept himself to himself. Maybe he had a heart attack and is dead in bed."

"We've been inside the property," Terry said. "He isn't there."

"When was the last time you saw him, sir?" DS Bill Pryor said.

"Must be about nine or ten days ago," Reg said. "He was pottering about in his garden."

"His niece tells us that he was supposed to be going to her wedding last Saturday, and that he was looking forward to it," Bill said. "So I think we can rule out the possibility of him just taking off."

Reg hiked his shoulders. "Beats me," he said. "Like I told you, we kept out of each other's way. Neither one of us had the need of company. That's probably why both of us live out in the sticks."

"Well, if he turns up, tell him to contact us, and his niece," Bill said, about to leave.

That was when fate in the shape of Claws trotted in through the cat flap, purring like an outboard motor, to stop in front of Bill and drop something at his feet.

Bill liked cats. He bent down to stroke Claws, but stopped with his hand an inch from the coal-black fur, to study the object next to his shoe.

Reg heard the loud intake of his own breath. The cat had never liked him. Was this its way of paying him back for too many slaps and kicks and insults? For the mangled article on the tiled floor in front of the copper was not a chewed up bird or mouse, but a discoloured and bloated finger, complete with nail.

Reg rightly assumed that this was not something he would be able to talk his way out of. On reflection, chopping Albert up into little pieces had not been one of his better ideas.

HOW WAS YOUR DAY?

"**OH** well, another day another dollar," Harry Turner said as he drained his mug, wincing at the bitter taste of the now cold coffee and blissfully unaware that a far worse experience was looming on the not too distant horizon.

"Why do you always say that, Dad? We live in Wood Green, not America."

"Because 'another day another pound' doesn't sound right, Pumpkin. Finish up your cereal and I'll drop you off at school."

"It's Sunday, Dad," Julie giggled. "You are seriously beginning to lose the plot."

Maybe I am, Harry thought. The days just seemed to tumble into each other with little to mark their passing. Time had become a strange and elastic medium to him. Could it really be almost four years since Kathy had been so cruelly taken from them, at the ripe old age of thirty-one, leaving him to somehow cope and bring up their daughter alone? Julie had been eight at the time, and with the resilience of youth had adjusted and let life carry her forward on the crest of its unstoppable wave. She had incorporated the loss, gone through the normal stages of grief, and moved on. He, on the other hand, was still in a cold, dark tunnel, though his love for Julie was slowly bringing him ever closer to the end of it, hopefully into warmth and light.

"I was just testing," he said, manufacturing a weak smile, which felt more like a grimace. "What have you got planned for today?"

"Uncle Peter and Auntie Claire are taking me to the zoo. You seem to be forgetting everything, Dad. I think you've got 'old timers' disease."

"You mean, Alzheimer's."

"Whatever."

"Well, have a good time. And don't get eaten by a crocodile."

"Why a crocodile? Why not a hungry hippo, or a peckish panther?"

He shrugged. "Because crocs have really bad breath, and they don't chew their food."

"You're funny, Dad," Julie said, going to him and giving him a big hug and a kiss on his cheek. "Ow! Your face is all scratchy, like sandpaper."

Half an hour later Kathy's sister and her husband arrived, breezing in and whisking Julie off to Regent's Park. Harry showered, shaved and then read the morning paper while he waited for his mobile to ring.

He was fortunate – given the situation – that his parents, in-laws and the rest of the family had willingly weighed-in and helped him to raise Julie. As a now single parent he had to continually juggle his life, with his daughter firmly the number one priority and consideration. And being a self-employed taxi driver helped. It gave him a certain amount of flexibility that a nine-to-five job would have precluded.

As a cabby, Harry thought he had seen it all, but was in for a surprise that day, and not of the pleasant variety. Over the years he had had his moments. His fares had included movie stars, sporting legends, rock idols and politicians. The rear seat of his taxi had supported the arses of the rich and famous, and had even had a baby delivered on it the previous year, as he failed to reach the hospital in time for the little chap to enter the world in a more orthodox setting.

All in all, Harry's chosen occupation was far from mundane, although of late his most notable fare had been the ferrying of a young female curate to a public house in Brentwood. She had asked him to wait, and then reappeared half an hour later, scantily clad and minus her dog collar. She had been followed into the car park by a horde of drunken revellers. The woman of the cloth was in fact a strippogram, who had escaped wearing little more than her birthday suit.

The phone trilled, and the manifestation of the shapely blonde evaporated from his mind.

"Turner's Taxis," he said.

"I need a cab for four, to take us from 17 Cavendish Road to Planet Graphics in Barnet."

"And your name, sir?"

"Kellog. How long will you be?"

"I can be there in ten minutes, Mr Kellog."

"We'll be waitin'."

None of the four male passengers spoke to each other or to him on the way to Barnet. And that was just fine. Conversation didn't come easy to Harry. He'd spent too many years making small talk about football, politics and the weather.

"Park up around back," Kellog – The Cornflake Kid – said as they reached their destination.

Harry duly pulled into a secluded and empty car park at the rear of the building.

"Magic," Cornflake said, leaning forward and pressing the barrels of a sawn-off shotgun against Harry's neck. "Now give me the keys and your phone and then sit back and relax."

Harry was a taxi driver, not a would-be hero. He passed the keys and his mobile over his shoulder, slowly, and wondered how something like this could be happening to him on such a bright summer's day.

The three other men – who could have been hotshot stockbrokers in their dark suits and polished shoes – climbed out of the car and headed back in the direction of the High Street.

"You want to know what's goin' down, am I right?" Jimmy Kellog, ex-con and self-proclaimed number one fan of the late Kray twins asked as he lowered the modified 12 gauge and jabbed it into the back of the drivers seat, to let Harry know that although out of sight, the weapon was now perfectly poised to turn his backbone into puree.

"No," Harry said. "My Mum always told me that ignorance is bliss."

"Two of the other guys are my colleagues," Jimmy continued, not content to keep his intended business a private matter. "And the other is the manager of the bank around the corner, who lives with his wife and kids at the address you picked us up at. I'm tellin' you all this because if anythin' goes wrong, then another of my associates, who is still at the house, will do them a serious mischief. Do you understand?"

Harry nodded and said, "Yes. I have no intention of giving you cause to harm me or anyone else."

"That's music to my ears, Harry."

Harry! How did he know his name?

"When the others come back, I want you to keep cool and follow my instructions. If you behave, you get to play another day. And I suggest that you be very vague when the plods ask you for descriptions of us. We know where you live, and you wouldn't want anythin' terrible to happen to Julie, would you?"

Harry's spine flash froze with fear. They had not phoned him by chance, but had done their homework and were covering all the bases. "You wore Balaclavas and spoke with foreign accents," he said.

"That's good thinkin', Harry. Now pull the boot release," Cornflake said, chuckling and handing the keys back as the others reappeared, to unceremoniously bundle the ashen-faced bank manager into the boot of the car.

Harry drove as directed to a lockup garage at the end of a derelict side street off India Dock Road, where once more his keys were taken from him.

Blindfolded and with a plastic tie pinioning his wrists, Harry was manhandled out of the car and pushed into the rear seat. The cold steel of the shotgun's barrels was rammed against the side of his neck, and he grunted in pain and fear, every muscle of his body tense, positive that this was it, and that he was going to be murdered in cold blood.

"Here's the plan," the now familiar voice of Cornflake said as Harry heard a vehicle start up and pull out of the garage. "We leave you and the other bozo in the lockup, in your cab. We drive away, and that's it. There's a couple of grand in the glove compartment for your time and trouble. I suggest that you two get your story straight before you get free and call the Old Bill. Just don't risk everythin' you care about by runnin' off at the mouth. If either of you describe us it will be members of your families that will wind up in the mortuary. Bye, Harry."

It took Harry quite a long time to chew his way through the tough plastic. He then removed the blindfold and saw that the car keys and his mobile were on the seat next to him. Unlocking the boot, he helped the bank manager, Simon Drury, out of it, and told him of the threat that Cornflake had made.

"I've got a wife and three children," Simon said. "I have no intention of putting their lives at risk. What do you suggest we tell the police?"

It was past nine in the evening before the police finally released Harry and Simon, after they had given the same statement a dozen times to as many different officers. Harry's car had been impounded, and was now in the hands of a forensic team, whom Harry had no doubt would find hundreds of worthless prints, and a wealth of assorted hair and fibre samples, due to it being used as a cab.

"What happened, Dad? Are you all right?" Julie said, rushing to the door as her aunt opened it.

"Make me a cup of coffee, Pumpkin, and I'll tell you the whole story," he lied.

Walking into the kitchen, he stopped dead in his tracks as a news flash regarding the bank raid in Barnet appeared on the portable TV.

"…It has been confirmed," said the stony-faced talking head, who was standing in front of a dramatic backdrop of twisted metal and the flashing blue lights of emergency service vehicles, "that during a high speed chase, a stolen car being used by suspected bank robbers crashed, killing all three occupants. A rucksack containing the money stolen from a bank in Barnet has been recovered..."

Harry slumped into a chair, consumed by a dizzying sense of relief. Sometimes it took the threat of fresh loss to bring home just how much you have. He suddenly felt that he could move forward, cherish the memory of Kathy, and also embrace the present and plan for the future.

"So, tell me everything," Julie said, placing a steaming mug of coffee in front of him.

"You first, Pumpkin," he countered. "How was your day? Did you run into any foul-breathed old crocodiles or hungry hippos?"

A LASTING IMPRESSION

IT was almost seven o'clock on a sticky August evening when the unmarked police car pulled into the kerb behind other official vehicles that were parked on the tree-lined avenue.

Climbing out of the Sierra, Detective Inspector Matt Barnes flicked his cigarette butt onto the verge, grinding it under the sole of his western-style boot, to then step carefully around the piles of dog shit, which littered the sun-killed yellow grass between the road and pavement like landmines. He was hot, tired, and could feel the perspiration at the small of his back and armpits. His casual, open-necked shirt stuck to him like flypaper, and his jeans felt damp. He needed to be home with Beth; to maybe take a shower with her, and then savour a large Scotch over ice, followed by a few hours' much needed sleep.

This scene that he was attending, with Detective Sergeant Pete Deakin in tow, was probably an accidental death, pure and simple. But he always approached a scene with the view that a crime *had* been committed. He was a cynical bastard with a slightly jaundiced view of his fellow man; believing that society was basically corrupt and that the individuals within it – including himself – were to a greater or lesser extent morally bankrupt, and therefore capable of any and all extremes of behaviour, given the right circumstances and corner to fight.

The young uniform at the door recognised him. "The deceased is upstairs, sir, in the bathroom," he said.

Matt nodded and entered the house, to be met by Sergeant Julie Gibson, the Crime Scene Coordinator, who gave Matt and Pete terse smiles, as well as cellophane gloves and plastic booties to wear

"What's the story?" Matt said, forgoing any small talk.

"It's just tragic, guv. Doesn't look like one for us," Julie replied, thinking that with his overlong dark hair and chiselled features the DI looked more like a movie star than a copper: shades of George Clooney. "A woman taking a bath with a radio plugged into the mains. They say oil and water don't mix, but in this case it was electricity and water."

"Show me."

Julie led them up the stairs, across a narrow landing and into the bathroom. They stood and took in the scene; absorbed it. The corpse almost filled the bath. She was an extremely large woman, who brought to Matt's mind the image of one of the hippos from The Dance of the Hours in Disney's Fantasia, or a jumble of swollen, pink party balloons breaking the rose-scented surface. Her glazed, pale blue eyes stared up through the water, as though examining the Artex whorls on the ceiling above. Her mouth was a rictus maw; tongue protruding rudely from between Colgate-white teeth. Not a pretty sight. The radio/cassette player was still in the tub, with the extension cable plugged into it.

Matt sat on the wooden toilet seat, took a crumpled pack of cigarettes from a pocket of his timeworn leather blouson and fired one up, to take a deep drag and blow a perfect ring of blue smoke up towards the mirror facing him above the wash hand basin. After a minute's contemplation, he stood up, lifted the lid and flicked the half-smoked Superking into the bowl. Julie was not impressed. The DI contaminated crime scenes with little regard for the techies who would soon be crawling all over the place like fleas on a feral dog.

Scratching his unshaven cheek, Matt followed the snaking flex out of the bathroom and into the adjacent bedroom, where the plug had been removed from the power socket. Pete and Julie tagged along behind him.

"What was her name?" Matt said, moving around the room inspecting every surface. His gimlet eyes were the grey of church-roof lead, and gave no insight as to his thoughts or mood. If he had emotions, they were kept under tight wraps.

"Vanessa Whitfield," Julie said. "Her husband, Raymond, is downstairs."

"Let's go talk to him," Matt said, heading for the landing.

Raymond was sitting on the settee in the lounge; head sagging down between his bony shoulders, hands cradling his face; grief personified.

"Excuse me, Mr Whitfield," Matt said, sitting opposite the man, with a glass-topped coffee table between them. Julie and Pete just stood and listened.

With his knuckles wiping tears from red-rimmed eyes, Raymond looked up, blinking rapidly as he faced Matt. His countenance was a picture of misery and almost palpable pain, and his trembling hands clenched and unclenched without pause.

"I'm sorry for your loss," Matt said. "But I need to ask you a couple of questions, sir. I won't keep you long." And to Julie. "Can you rustle up some coffee, black?"

Julie nodded and left the room. She didn't really know Barnes all that well, but had taken a dislike to the brusque DI, who she adjudged to be as sociable as a grizzly bear suffering from irritable bowel syndrome, haemorrhoids, or both.

"Did you find your wife, sir?" Matt said.

Raymond nodded slowly, not making eye contact, but now staring fixedly at the TV and DVD remotes on the tabletop.

"Run through it in your own time," Matt said.

After a pause, Raymond began to talk in a whisper. "I...I got home from work at five-thirty. I could smell the bubble bath, so I knew that V...Vanessa was upstairs. I walked through to the kitchen and switched on the kettle, and then went up to change. When I called her, there was no reply. I...I found her in the bath and called for an ambulance. That's it."

"Did you unplug the extension in the bedroom?" Matt said, not even acknowledging Julie as she placed a tray with four mugs of coffee on the coasters in front of them.

"Yes. But it was too late. I could see that Vanessa was...was dead," Raymond sniffled.

"Why would she use the mains electric, sir? Didn't she know the danger?" Matt said.

Raymond shrugged. "I told her not to, dozens of times. She liked to listen to music when she took a bath. The batteries in the radio must have been dead."

Matt lit another cigarette without asking if it was okay. He elected to smoke anywhere, if he could get away with it, and was not easily discouraged by non-smokers. They didn't shout so loud about the effects from industrial pollution, or the toxic exhaust fumes pumped into the atmosphere by cars and planes, turning the air to shit on a stick. Jesus! London would soon be as smogged-up as LA or Tokyo.

"Whereabouts was the radio usually kept?" Matt said before sipping some of the strong, hot coffee.

"It was always on the windowsill in the bathroom," Raymond said.

"And the extension lead?"

"The bedroom, in the bottom of the wardrobe."

"I noticed a glass in the bathwater, sir."

"Vanessa liked brandy, a lot. I imagine she took one up with her."

"Was it a problem?"

"Well...yes. She drank too much."

"Why?"

"We lost a baby. It was a cot death. She couldn't have another. That was ten years ago. It affected her badly. She started drinking and it got out of hand."

"That's all for now, sir. I'm sorry if we've caused you any undue stress," Matt said, his voice monotone, without a trace of compassion. He left the room, jerking his head for Pete and Julie to follow him.

"Clear cut, eh?" Julie said as they left the house and walked over to the car, where Pete got in the passenger side. "Not a crime scene."

"You reckon?" Matt said.

Julie nodded. "Yes. I think it's obvious that the deceased had been drinking, and then went to take a bath. The batteries in the radio were dead, so she used the extension. She must have knocked the radio into the water and been electrocuted."

Matt shook his head. "She's a murder victim. We're looking for a girlfriend. The bereaved is putting on a good act, but he topped his wife. It wasn't an accident or suicide. He wanted out of an unhappy marriage, but wasn't prepared to walk and lose the house and everything else."

"There's no evidence to suggest or support any of that, sir," Julie said, sure that the jaded looking DI was trying to make a big deal out of what to her was nothing more than a sad and fatal accident.

"Just make sure that the photographer takes shots of the windowsill in the bathroom, and the top of the dressing table in the bedroom," Matt said, climbing into the car, starting it up and accelerating away without waiting for an answer.

"Obnoxious pig!" Julie said aloud, feeling the heat rise in her cheeks as she decided that despite his reputation for closing cases he was an ignorant and misguided tosser.

It was four days before Matt was ready to talk to Whitfield again. This time in the formal surroundings of an interview room at the station.

Police work was gathering evidence and facts, to then interpret them and prove or discount the likelihood of a crime having been committed, and more importantly, to lead them to the offender. Matt had studied the police, forensic and autopsy reports; the works. He had also followed up his own line of inquiry. Now, having invited Sergeant Julie Gibson to attend and sit in on the interview with Raymond Whitfield, and with the tapes running, he faced the still mournful looking suspect across a cigarette-scarred table, which was bolted to the concrete floor directly under the flat light that shone down from a naked and fly-shit spotted fluorescent tube.

Sipping coffee in the claustrophobic surroundings, Matt gave Raymond a steely glare that might have curdled milk, and then said with a thin, knowing smile on his face, "Thank you for coming in this morning, Mr Whitfield. I just need to go over one or two points with you."

"No problem," Raymond said. "But why are you interviewing me again? I thought it was clear that Vanessa's death was a terrible accident."

"Not necessarily, sir. When there are ambiguities, such as you having a mistress, then we have to investigate all possibilities."

Raymond's silence and stunned expression were an admission of his extramarital affair with Helen Brewer, his secretary.

"So, let's get back to when you arrived home that day," Matt said.

"I've already told you. I went straight into the kitchen, switched on the kettle and then went upstairs and found Vanessa. I unplugged the extension and phoned for help. That's it."

"Strange that the incident didn't blow the fuses," Matt said, enjoying the sight of Whitfield visibly squirming in the plastic contour chair. "And why didn't you pull your wife out of the bath and try to resuscitate her?"

"I...I tried. You saw her. She was too heavy. And I could see that she was dead, for Christ's sake."

"When the paramedics arrived, they noted that your clothes were bone dry, sir."

"What are you saying?"

"That you lied at the scene, and you're lying now," Matt said. "You planned and then carried out the murder of your wife in cold blood."

"You can't prove that," Raymond shouted, bringing both of his fists down on the tabletop.

Matt didn't flinch. "You took perfectly good batteries out of the radio and replaced them with dead ones. You then plugged the radio into the extension, turned it on, walked into the bathroom and threw it in the tub, electrocuting your wife.

When you were sure that she was dead, you turned the juice off and phoned the emergency services."

"Screw you. I don't have to listen to this rubbish," Raymond seethed through clenched teeth, pushing the chair back and shooting to his feet.

"That's where we found the original batteries, with your fingerprints on them, Whitfield. At the bottom of a bin bag in your wheelie bin, to be precise. Who would throw perfectly good batteries away? Oh, and the radio had not been on the windowsill or anywhere else in the bathroom. With the condensation it would have left an impression. What we did find was an outline of it in the dust on the dresser top in the bedroom, which doesn't tie in with your story of it always being in the bathroom.

"I...I think—"

"That you need a lawyer, Mr Whitfield," Matt said. "Because I'm now going to formally charge you with the murder of your wife, and read you your rights."

Out in the sunlight, Matt walked down the street to the Starbucks on the corner. He went inside and asked Gina behind the counter for a large cup of strong black coffee, before going back outside to sit at an umbrella-shaded pavement table. He yawned, fumbled in his pocket for cigarettes, but changed his mind. Maybe he would give up the habit, again. He had tried to several times, but the addiction wouldn't let go, yet.

There was no rest for the wicked, or cops. His phone rang, and one of the team told him that a headless corpse had been washed up on the mud at the side of the Thames in Putney. It was the second to be found in the space of three weeks. Maybe some psycho serial killer who got off on The Legend of Sleepy Hollow was starting up. His squad had been given the case.

"You were right, guv," Julie Gibson said, appearing at his side. "I must admit, I thought you were way off track."

He shrugged. "You want a cup of coffee, Julie? I'm buying."

"Yeah, latte," she said, taking a seat. She now thought that Matt Barnes was just a little distant and insular, but not obnoxious. He was good at what he did, and seemed driven. She had begun to find him very enigmatic, had quizzed his sidekick DS Pete Deakin about him, and Pete had told her that Barnes was off limits; in a heavy relationship with a psychologist. And that was fine. Julie realized that for some reason she was glad. Matt Barnes would probably have been far too much for her to handle if he'd not been spoken for, and if she *had* made a play for him.

A few minutes later Matt drained his cup and stood up: "I've got to go," he said to Julie. "Seems murder is a lot like me, it doesn't take a holiday."

A BREACH OF TRUST

DEVON Davis was in the back of an old bottle-green Volkswagen transporter panel van that had decals for plumbing services on each side of it, and a set of ladders strapped to a roof rack. It was a vehicle that no one would give a second look.

Jay-Jay was driving. Carl Lincoln was sitting next to him, and Devon was under a tarp behind them, blindfolded, gagged, and with his wrists and ankles bound.

They stopped outside the gates of the facility, which was in a rundown area of Paddington at the side of derelict land that had been scheduled for redevelopment for over a decade.

Carl got out, unlocked the rusted wire mesh gates and pushed them sideways to bump and squeak as the wheels rolled on the recessed steel runners set into the crumbling concrete.

Jay-Jay drove in, turned left, and then first right into the second wide aisle, to park outside unit 43. Carl closed the gates and walked to the unit. There was no security guard, just a defunct camera at the gates. Most of the units were empty. This was a company owned by Dewey Daniels, and was a legitimate investment. The land that the storage units were on would make him a fortune when all the planning for proposed development was passed. It was a prime location.

Carl opened the roll-up door and then helped Jay-Jay lift Devon out of the back of the van and carry him into the unit to dump unceremoniously on the cement floor. The interior was the size of a regular garage. It had whitewashed breezeblock walls discoloured by large patches of almost black mould, and the only contents were: a metal table, two plastic contour chairs, a wall-mounted cupboard, and a large galvanised steel bucket with a mop and two scrubbing brushes in it, standing in a corner.

Carl squatted down, grasped Devon by his shirt and trousers and rolled him over to the wall, before going back out to the van to fetch a plastic sheet, which he unfolded and spread out on the floor.

Devon was terrified. They had lifted him as he had been standing outside the rear door of the massage parlour having a smoke. Jay-Jay had got out of the Volkswagen, said hi, and then hit him once, hard on the point of his jaw. He had been almost knocked unconscious, and collapsed as his legs turned to jelly and gave out on him. Seconds later he had been thrown into the rear of the van, to be gagged and have a sack that smelled of onions pulled over his head, and plastic ties used to bind his wrists and ankles. He was now stretched out on a cold hard surface, and from the sound of the rollup door being opened and closed, he thought he might be in a garage.

He had been fucking stupid; should have known that his scam would be found out at some point in time. But he'd needed extra cash to feed his personal drug habit.

It was ninety minutes later when Dewey Daniels arrived. He had showered and then dressed in a long sleeved cream chambray shirt, black leather jacket, blue jeans, and Dr Martens safety boots with steel toecaps. He parked his silver Mercedes outside the gates, let himself in, walked around to the unit and rapped on the door. Carl rolled it up just far enough for Dewey to duck under, and then closed it again.

The overhead fluorescent tube had no casing, and its flat, bright light was reflected back from the shiny black plastic.

"Take the bag off his head," Dewey said, and Jay-Jay did, and removed the gag.

Devon squinted against the light, blinking rapidly before turning his head to face Dewey. "I'm sorry, boss," he said. "I'll pay you back and make it right, I swear to God I will."

Dewey pulled up one of the chairs, and before sitting down in front of the young man, he said, "No, Devon, *I'll* make it right, and drove his left leg forward, for the steel toecap of his boot to slam into Devon's side, snapping two ribs under the impact.

The scream that Devon emitted was not particularly loud, but relayed the agony that he was now in. It flashed through his mind that he could well be killed where he lay. Six months ago, one of the girls, Cheryl, who whored for Dewey, had started freelancing on the side to make a few extra quid, and word of mouth had it that she had been garrotted and wound up in the foundations of what was now a new office block in the city. She had done the same thing before, had been severely beaten, and given a warning to behave, but had obviously been too stupid to take heed of it.

"The amount of money that you took isn't important, son," Dewey said as he sat forward on the chair with his forearms on his thighs. "It's all about principle, loyalty, and not taking the piss out of someone who gave you his trust. You had a cush job, just watching over the girls at the parlour and making sure that none of the punters got out of hand. Ha, out of hand. That's funny. We provide services. I want the guys that use the parlours to leave happy and come back for more. The going rate for a massage with H E is thirty quid. You told three of the girls to up it to forty-five, and then you split the difference with them. Fortunately, one of them was sensible enough to know that you'd get sussed, so she gave Jay-Jay a call."

H E stood for Happy Ending, which involved a punter being given a hand or blow job after receiving a perfunctory body massage. Devon had thought it was a sweet little scam. The girls couldn't very well admit the arrangement. And they were afraid of Devon; knew that he had an evil temper, and were sure that he had been involved with whatever had happened to the girl that had gone missing, though in fact he had not.

"I was up to my neck in debt, boss," Devon said in a whiny voice.

Dewey lashed out with his boot again, this time to connect with Devon's thigh, but only hard enough to deaden the muscle, not fracture the femur.

Devon screamed and curled up, expecting more pain to follow.

Dewey took a stainless steel nine-millimetre Browning pistol from a pocket of his jacket and aimed it at Devon's head.

There followed a profound silence. Devon eventually looked up at Dewey again and started shaking his head as he was faced by the muzzle of the gun pointing at his forehead.

"Please, boss, don't shoot me," Devon said.

"Too late to beg for your life," Dewey said. "You're like a rotten apple in a barrel. You need to be got rid of. You've abused my trust. Get up on your knees."

Devon struggled up into a kneeling position. He was trembling like a leaf in the wind and wanted to close his eyes, but couldn't. He was mesmerised by the gun that he knew was about to spit a bullet out and blow the brains out of the back of his head. It crossed his mind that he would in all likelihood feel nothing; just be dead and gone, as if he'd never been.

There wasn't much slack on the trigger. Dewey applied a little extra pressure with his thick, hairy index finger and fired.

Devon jerked backwards, and heard the metallic click. There had been no bullet in the chamber.

Dewey, Jay-Jay and Carl chuckled.

Devon shit in his pants.

"How does it feel to meet death head on and survive it?" Dewey said as he pocketed the gun.

Devon didn't reply; just threw up on the plastic sheet.

"That's the one and only break I'm ever gonna give you," Dewey said. "And to get back on side and put this behind us, I want you to do a special job for me.

It was on the Friday evening ten days after the nightmare episode in the unit at the storage facility in Paddington that Devon got the call from Jay-Jay.

"Time to take care of that special job that the boss wants you to deal with," Jay-Jay said. "Meet me at the end of your street in half an hour."

Jay-Jay was already there, sitting behind the wheel of a black Discovery that had no doubt been stolen and run through one of Dewey's chop shops to have the engine number and other ID on it altered.

Devon climbed in the passenger side and groaned as he put the seat belt on. His cracked ribs were taped up, but still hurt.

"What's the job?" Devon said.

"I drive you to the end of an avenue in Camden Town and give you a shooter, and you go to number fifty-four and ring the doorbell. When the guy answers it you put two slugs in his head and make sure that he's dead."

"I've never topped anyone," Devon said.

"There's a first time for everything," Jay-Jay said. "You do this without a hitch and you get a clean sheet with the boss. Could even be a move up the ladder, unless you'd rather keep on working at that poxy massage parlour."

"Who do I have to shoot?"

"A bent copper that has outlived his usefulness. The less you know the better. He's about forty years old, six-foot tall with broad-shoulders and black hair. Don't say a word to him, just blow him away. Okay?"

"Yeah," Devon said. "Will you be waiting for me?"

"I'll give you three minutes to get back to the car. Then I'm gone. If for any reason you fuck up, wipe the gun, ditch it in the canal and catch a tube back home. Then give me a bell."

Jay-Jay reached the end of the avenue and asked Devon to hand over his mobile phone, due to it having contact numbers in it that he didn't want to risk falling into the wrong hands. He then told Devon to open the glove box and take the old Sig-Sauer semiautomatic out of the ziplock bag it was in.

The modern semidetached house had a light on in the lounge. Devon took a few deep breaths and gripped the pistol tightly in his right hand as he used a knuckle of his left to push the doorbell.

An attractive woman in her thirties with mahogany hair hung loose to her shoulders opened the door. The gun that he had drawn was frozen in his hand. *Where was the fucking copper?*

He couldn't pull the trigger. Just stood there like a statue. And by the time he decided to just run away it was too late. The woman was pushed to one side, and behind her was a man that fitted the description Jay-Jay had given him. There was also a little girl peeking out from behind him.

The copper, DI John Clifford, just stood there and said, "Please don't harm my wife and daughter. It was as if he had been expecting an attempt on his life.

It was all too much for Devon. He was a small-time crook, not a hitman.

"Take a few steps back along the hall," Devon said to the man and his family as he entered the house, kicked the door closed behind him and said, "Who are you?" to the man.

John frowned. "Detective Inspector John Clifford," he said.

"I'm in deep shit and need your help, Inspector. "I was told to shoot you, but have no intention of doing it."

"Give me the gun, then," John said. And we'll talk about it."

Devon gave it some thought. He had all but signed his own death warrant. He could see two possible futures in front of him; one, being tortured and murdered and his body being fed through a wood chipper, or to pigs, because he had bottled out. The alternative was telling the copper everything he knew about Dewey Daniels' organisation, and hoping that Witness Protection and a new identity would be enough to give him a fresh start.

And then a third way of handling the situation came to mind. He kept the gun trained on the copper as he backed up to the door, to open it and slam it closed behind him as he ran from the house.

Failing to carry out the hit, through no fault of his own, would in all probability result in him being slapped around a little, which was perhaps the best he could hope for, given the circumstances. He would tell Jay-Jay that the copper had not been in, and that it had been his wife that came to the door.

Approximately a week later a photo of Devon Davis appeared on the News at Ten. It was reported that the body of the young man had been discovered on the banks of the Thames at Battersea, and that the death was subject to a murder inquiry. Details of the mutilation that had been inflicted on Devon had been withheld. A second breach of trust had not been tolerated.

KATHERINE & EDDIE

IT was mid-July and the aircon vent next to my desk was chugging out warm air, and the squad room was as hot as hell. I'd loosened my tie, unbuttoned my shirt collar and rolled the sleeves up to my elbows. Sweat was sticking my back to the swivel chair. I was tempted to just get up, walk out and ride the elevator down to street level. A cold beer or two at the nearby Redwood Bar and Grill was tempting. As it was I'd have to wait. Another fifteen minutes and I was due on the ninth floor to be evaluated by some broad that wouldn't know shit from Shinola if she fell into a bath of either. Ms. Katherine Moore was some kind of shrink with a lot of power in her Sharpie. Until she signed off on me I would be riding the desk on the sixth floor of Police Headquarters at 100 West 1st Street, picking at a keyboard with two fingers and feeling like a caged critter. Okay, it was routine; happened every time a cop discharged his firearm and wounded or killed someone in the line of duty. The rules said that the officer – or detective in my case – had to be officially assessed and passed as being psychologically fit before he was re-issued his gun and let loose again.

Folding my jacket over my shoulder and not bothering to fasten the collar of the now damp and clingy shirt, I went over to the cooler for a cup of water, and then walked along the corridor and took the stairs up to the ninth. The elevator car always had an underlying smell of cheap perfume, cheaper aftershave lotion and sweat.

She kept me waiting in an anteroom for ten minutes before opening her office door and giving me a smile that I was sure had the power to curdle milk.

"Come in, Detective Boyd," she said, somehow making the word detective sound unsavory, like a dead tuna fish rotting on a dock in the midday sun. "This shouldn't take too long."

To me that meant that I could be in the dragon's den for at least an hour, and my stomach was rumbling, crying out for a loaded burger and fries.

"And how are we today?"

We? "I'm fine," I said. "How are you?"

No answer. She just inclined her head to a chair in front of her highly polished hardwood desk, went behind it and parked her shapely ass.

"I'd like to start off by asking you how you've been coping since the incident that took place two weeks ago."

"So ask me."

Her lips pursed and became as narrow as a paper cut. I was being confrontational and knew it. Diplomacy had never been, and still wasn't, in my repertoire.

"I sense a little hostility," she said. "Do you have an issue that you want to share with me?"

"Hostility is a strong word, Ms. Moore," I said. "It implies that I'm being antagonistic or aggressive, which I'm not."

She flipped through a file in front of her, which I knew was my service record, and that it was peppered with commendations. She regrouped and found composure as she decided which way to go with her line of questioning.

"Okay, Detective," she said. "I note that you have been this route on five previous occasions in less than nine years."

"I'm a homicide detective. Sometimes shit happens and people die. I have always executed my duties in a professional manner, and have been found justified lawfully over each incident for the actions that I took. What more can I tell you?"

"How it affects you. Exactly how you feel after you have taken another human being's life."

"I've never discharged my weapon without it being a last resort, to protect and serve, as the saying goes."

"A lot of officers find difficulties in assimilating that kind of experience," she said. "They have problems sleeping, or turn to alcohol, or—"

"I don't have any problems with having done my duty," I said. "This is my twenty-second year with the LAPD. I'm forty-five years old, drink bourbon in moderation, smoke cigarettes, am divorced, and happy in my own skin. The teenager that I shot a couple of weeks ago had just gunned down the manager of a 7-Eleven store on Fairfax. My partner and I were just a couple of blocks away. We arrived within seconds. The perp was still in the store. He'd taken the bills and loose change from the register and was helping himself to other stuff when we entered and told him to drop the Saturday-night special that he was still holding. He ignored us and took a pot-shot. The bullet hit my partner in the shoulder, and so I opened fire."

"And that doesn't have an effect on you?"

"I guess it does. It saddens me that the manager of the store, Bernie Pasco, a fifty-six year old married guy with four children never got to go home again. That I shot the punk who splashed his brains over the door of a display cabinet doesn't bring Bernie back, but it sure as hell doesn't make me feel guilty or disturbed by what I did."

Katherine Moore just looked at me for several seconds without saying a word. I almost said to her, 'What if Bernie had been your husband or father?', but decided that I didn't really give a flying fuck what she thought or how she felt. She was just doing her job, and probably lived out in the Valley and had never been mugged, beaten up or raped. But what did I know? She was just an obstacle stopping me from getting back out on the street with my Glock 17 in its holster.

"You want a cup of coffee," she said, eventually, and almost gave me a real smile, which made her look several years younger and a lot prettier.

"Black," I said, noting that she did not wear a wedding band.

We had two cups each and got to talking on first name terms about Trump and the state of the nation, and other lighter stuff. We both liked the Boss, Springsteen. She had lightened up and become more of a real person to me. An hour passed like a New York minute. Maybe she was playing me, but I didn't think so. I'd spent too many years on mean streets to be taken in, I hoped.

"Let's meet up next week, same time same place, Eddie," Katherine said. "I don't see there being a problem. You've got your shit together, Detective."

I grinned. There was a lot more to Katherine Moore than initially met the eye. She had grown on me, big-time.

"Maybe when we get this business settled we can meet up for a meal," I said. "How does that sound?"

"Sounds like a plan," Katherine said.

I walked back down the stairwell whistling an old Merle Haggard song that came into my head: 'That's The Way Love Goes'. Funny how you could meet a person for the first time and be smitten. Maybe it was just lust at first sight. I was already visualizing having a steak meal with Katherine at the Trocadero Lounge on the strip, and maybe seeing her again…and again.

LIKE TAKING CANDY...

"**TRUST** me Johnny," Nick said, pausing to wipe at the perspiration that ran down his flushed face like rain on a window pane, even though the ground beyond the partly raised door of the garage was sparkling with December frost. "It'll be a walk in the park, I guarantee it. We get inside the guy's house an' hold the woman an' kids hostage while he goes to the bank an' gets the money."

"No violence, huh?" Johnny said, a little apprehensive at the sight of the old Mossberg shotgun that Nick had in a vice and was laboriously hack-sawing off the greater part of both barrels, having already shortened the wooden stock.

Nick resumed sawing. "No sweat, Johnny. This is just to put the frighteners on 'em. I might not even load it. I've told you, we wear Balaclavas over our heads and disguise our voices. Once we've got the dosh, we leave 'em tied up an' take off. Nothin' can go wrong."

"What if he refuses to do it?"

"He won't. This is a bank manager an' his family, not a bunch of Marines with M16s."

"I dunno," Johnny mumbled, looking out through the grime-coated window of the garage, towards the grey factory chimney that belched even greyer smoke up into the gunmetal clouds of a winter sky.

"Relax," Nick said, flinching and jumping back as the heavy steel barrels fell to the concrete floor with the clanging sound of church bells.

"You said relax last time, remember, an' we spent six months inside for stealin' that copper cable from the railway," Johnny said.

"This is a cert; a piece of cake like my mum used to bake. I told you, Charlie Dawson uses this guy's bank an' says he's a spineless Muppet. He has a photo of his wife an' kids on his desk, and talks about 'em at the drop of a hat. He ain't gonna risk 'em gettin' topped over money that doesn't belong to him."

"So when do we do it?" Johnny said, lighting a cigarette and sitting on the old, ripped and stained settee that squatted like a battle-worn pit-bull against the rough, breezeblock wall.

"Thursday night," Nick said as he filed the sharp edges off the ends of the now shortened barrels. "I'll meet you in the Black Bull at eight."

Johnny had known Nick since they had both been snot-nosed kids. They had fought their way up in the backstreets of the East End, where no quarter was asked for or given. Nick had always been a bad influence, whose heroes were gangsters, or long dead actors who'd portrayed them. He was also a fan of Robert De Niro, who he thought had played a great psycho as Max Cade in the remake of the movie *Cape Wrath*. Johnny grinned. He remembered Nick stalking the star for his autograph when he had been in London for a premiere. He never did get it. Most showbiz types thought every fan might turn out to be a Mark Chapman, and they didn't want their tickets punched the way John Lennon's had been. There were memories of some good times as teenagers, though, but in the main Johnny's many troubles had stemmed from being drawn into Nick's crazy schemes, that with few exceptions had ended in disaster, and usually with a probation order or a short stretch inside. Not that he could dump all the blame at Nick's booted feet. He was always up for making a few quid, but was also scared of his powerfully built pal and his violent disposition, which bubbled just beneath the surface of the outwardly amiable personality he projected.

Although easily led, Johnny – at twenty-nine – was finally wising up. If this job worked out, he would take his cut and drive up north. He knew a guy in Manchester who he had once shared a cell with in Strangeways. He was smart enough to know that if he hung round with Nick long enough he would probably end up doing life. Nick liked guns, and was not afraid to use them. Being institutionalised to a degree was one thing, but the thought of growing old and maybe dying in a maximum security prison brought a solid, cold lump to Johnny's throat and made his stomach do back-flips. He was now in a relationship with a cute little nurse who worked at the West Middlesex Hospital, and didn't want to risk losing her. She thought he was a dead ringer for Brad Pitt, how the guy had looked twenty years ago, and he reckoned that was cool. She also thought he had a regular job as a security guard out at Heathrow, but he didn't. He just hoped that she would go up north with him.

The balaclava and rubber gloves burned a hole in his pocket, so to speak, as Johnny listened to Wacko Jacko singing Smooth Criminal on the jukebox and nervously sipped at a pint of lager.

"All set?" Nick said, draining his glass and getting up from the stool at the bar, impatient to do the business.

Feather light flakes of snow were drifting down and beginning to carpet the pavement when they left the pub. They hunched their shoulders against the cold and hurried along the pavement, to turn into a dimly lit back street and climb into a Ford Mondeo that Nick had hotwired earlier that evening.

Johnny got behind the wheel and drove across town, through west London and out to a tree-lined network of suburban avenues that abutted onto the southernmost fringe of a large park near Hounslow, having stopped once on the way at the rear of a vacant petrol station to switch plates, before cruising the neighbourhood and parking a quarter of a mile from their intended destination.

It was gone eleven when they strolled past the house on Walnut Avenue.

"This is it," Nick said, looking both ways to satisfy himself that no late-night dog-walkers, joggers or carol singers were in the vicinity, before vaulting over a wall and hunkering down behind snow-topped laurel and other lush evergreens that screened him from sight of the street. Johnny joined him, grunting as the sharp spines of holly leaves scratched his cheek.

They lingered for a few minutes, listening, waiting for their night vision to adapt to the gloom that was not penetrated by the sodium glare of streetlamps, and glad of the thick, low cloud cover and falling snow that shielded them from an unseen moon above.

They had all the privacy they needed. These were all differentiated dwellings, each insulated from its neighbours' by high fences, walls, or stands of trees; mainly conifers. The isolation that these residents' had created for themselves had rendered them vulnerable, as it also afforded cover for undesirable and uninvited trespassers.

Making their way up the edge of the sweeping drive, Johnny marvelled at the size of the front garden that was as big as a football field, and which he imagined the owners would probably refer to as 'the grounds'. He was also fascinated by the array of brightly coloured lights that festooned the house, and also an immense fir tree that was draped with twinkling white bulbs, heralding the fact that this was the week of Christmas.

After they had both pulled on Balaclavas and latex gloves, Nick thumbed the bell push and drew the sawn-off shotgun from beneath his parka and waited.

Lynne Bentley opened the door, but only to the extent that the security chain would allow. By the light from the hall she saw the dark, hooded face, with just mean, narrow eyes glaring out at her. She reacted quickly, attempted to slam the door back into its frame, but was a split second too late.

Nick lunged forward, and the impact of his shoulder ripped the chain's fittings from the wood, which splintered and gave under brute force. The door sprang back and the woman behind it was knocked sprawling onto her backside. Nick giggled as her legs flew up and the bottom of the towelling robe she wore flapped back to expose fleshy thighs and bright-red panties with motifs of green Christmas trees on them.

"Where are the kids?" Nick mumbled through the wads of cotton wool in his mouth, which padded his cheeks and distorted his voice behind the woollen helmet that hugged his face; a combination that made for a passable impression of the way Brando had sounded as Corleone in *The Godfather*, and how the average environmental activist or terrorist looked, hiding their features to escape recognition.

"They…They're upstairs asleep," Lynne said as she was jerked roughly to her feet and led into the living room, from where Edward Bentley had been rushing, only to stop in his tracks at the sight of the gun's barrels pointing at his wife's head.

"Go an' get 'em," Nick said to Lynne.

"But—"

"No buts, sweetheart. Just go with my friend an' bring the kids downstairs."

Edward took a step forward, but Nick rammed the twin muzzles up against Lynne's neck, shook his head and clucked his tongue at the infuriated but terrified man.

"Sit down, dummy, or the little lady gets to be dead," Nick said, knowing that he could control the situation with the right level of menace; an art that he had, in the main, consciously copied from watching so many old gangster movies.

The children were no problem. At three and five years old they thought it was a game and were happy to be allowed to be up so late. Johnny found a Disney DVD, put it on for them, and with cans of coke and a packet of chocolate biscuits that he got from the kitchen, they were happy campers. Both of them fell asleep less than twenty minutes into *The Lion King*.

It was a long night for Edward and Lynne. They were gagged, their wrists and ankles were tightly bound with duct tape, and they had no idea why their house had been invaded, or why they were being held hostage. If their assailants were burglars, then why hadn't they just ransacked the house and left?

As dawn broke, Nick ripped the tape from their mouths and spoke to Edward. "It's like this, my friend," he said. "You're goin' to drive to work as usual. I want you to go inside, act as though you haven't got a care in the world, an' bring out a couple of hundred grand at least, without raisin' suspicion. When you get back here with it, we leave you all tied up an' bugger off. It's that simple."

"But—"

"Shut up," Nick shouted, waving the shotgun in the air. "Don't say another fuckin' word. Just do exactly what you're told to or I swear to God I'll decorate the walls with your kids' brains."

"What if he goes to the cops, or just doesn't come back?" Johnny said.

Nick thought it over and paced up and down the room, before pulling his mask off and spitting the sodden wads of cotton wool out onto the carpet. His face was filmed with sweat, and his pale-blue eyes had a slightly crazed look to them.

"So I'll go with him," Nick said, picking up a mobile phone from the coffee table and handing the sawn-off to Johnny. "I'll call you every fifteen minutes. If I don't, shoot 'em all."

"They've seen your face, now." Johnny said.

"It doesn't matter. They haven't seen yours. If they say anythin' to the Old Bill after we've gone, an' I get lifted, then you can pay 'em another visit an' settle up. They'd never know when they were goin' to be blown away."

"We won't say anything, ever," Lynne said with tears misting her eyes. "Just don't hurt any of us, please."

With Johnny guarding the others, Nick left the house with Edward and told him to drive to his place of work in his Vectra. The plan had been slightly modified, but this was still a sweet little number that he had every intention of repeating. It was money for old rope. They had someone else stealing the cash for them and just handing it over. It was like taking candy from a baby, just as he'd known it would be.

Lighting a cigarette, Nick switched on the radio and hummed along to Bing Crosby singing *White Christmas*, as Edward drove slowly through the snow-covered streets.

Nick was already planning on what he'd do with the money. Nothing could go wrong. He would spend Christmas abroad with some of the proceeds from this caper. Maybe ask Rita – the stacked blonde waitress at the Black Bull – if she fancied a couple of weeks in Florida. Sex, sun, sand and fun in the Sunshine State would hit the spot. He had only ever been overseas once, to Spain, and that had been the previous summer. Florida in winter would be far better, because British winters were a pain in the arse. It would be the good life from here on in. His only regret was that he hadn't thought of doing this before. He and Johnny had always been small-time, but were now about to join the big league.

He checked in with Johnny as arranged and told him that everything was A-okay. It was all bluff. Johnny hadn't got the guts to shoot a sewer rat, never mind a woman and her children. But the wimp sitting next to him didn't know that, and it was fear for his family's well-being that guaranteed success.

"What the hell do you think you're doin'?" Nick said as the Vectra pulled to a stop outside some shop and Edward switched off the engine. "This ain't the bank. Why've you stopped here?"

Edward suddenly realised the terrible mistake that had been made; one that had placed his family in mortal danger. "Bank! You think I'm with the bank?" he said, staring at the brawny but mentally lightweight young hoodlum seated next to him.

Nick frowned, and the cogs turned slowly in his mind as he tried to make sense of what was going down.

"I run a print shop, you idiot," Edward shouted, his face bright red with anger. "My next door neighbour is a bank manager. You picked the wrong bloody house."

THE BLACK FEDORA HAT

IT was almost dawn, and every surface was coated in a layer of frost that sparkled under a waxing moon. The black velvet heavens were studded with the pinpricks of light from a billion stars which soon appeared to fade as the encroaching light diminished them from sight.

He stood outside the open door as still as a pillar of rock and gazed up as the Earth spun in monotonous orbit around the sun, where night and day took turns to envelop a portion of it. An owl hooted nearby, and a light breeze whispered through the bare branches of trees that clustered around the manor house, swaying in the way that kelp will in shallow seas as it is wafted this way and that by unseen currents and tides.

Edwin Morton was neither warm nor cold, hungry or thirsty, just content to be whom he was and where he lived; a solitary individual silhouetted in the doorway, alone with his dark thoughts and many memories of times gone by. He was of indeterminate age, with long white hair reaching his shoulders from beneath the wide brim of the fedora-style hat that was placed on his head at a jaunty angle. He also wore an ankle-length woollen greatcoat over a suit with extremely wide jacket lapels and twenty-two inch trouser bottoms complete with turn ups; the height of men's fashion in this year of the *believers'* Lord, nineteen thirty-five.

As the first tinge of pinkness stroked the land, Edwin turned, walked into the house and closed and locked the solid oak door. He made his way along a wide hallway, to enter a windowless study lit only by two large oil lamps, by the light of which he could sit behind a Jacobean desk and resume his daily task of writing on a state of the art Olympia typewriter, flexing his long, pale fingers before commencing to tap the glass-topped nickel keys and start a new chapter of the novel he was working on.

Jonas Carter came across the body at a little after eight a.m. as he cycled from his cottage along Snuff Mill Lane towards Kettlethorpe, where he worked as a clerk for the only solicitor in the small market town.

The corpse was lying supine in the withered grass with one arm bent at the elbow; the hand clawed as if it had been grasping at something in the air. Jonas almost fell off his bike at the sight, and shakily alighted and walked across the rutted surface of the lane and stared down, to be met by wide-open brown eyes that were glazed and unseeing. He did not have the need to check for a pulse, for the young woman was clearly beyond any help, still gripped by the rigor mortis that had caused a stiffening of the joints and muscles of the body to occur. And frost was adhered to her face and arms, which to his reckoning suggested that she had lain there lifeless for several hours.

"My God!" Jonas whispered as he recognised her. It was Emily Huggate, the daughter of the landlord of the Carpenter's Arms on King Street, which stood just a few paces from where Jonas worked.

He could see no visible wounds, and the girl appeared to be fully dressed. Perhaps she had been taken by a massive stroke or some other malady that resulted in sudden death. He needed to report his find, so took off on his bicycle along the lane at breakneck speed, not stopping until he reached the police station on High Street, gasping for breath as he staggered through the door on aching legs and made his way across to where a burly sergeant was standing behind his desk reading a newspaper and drinking tea from an overlarge and stained mug.

"You're as red in the face as a boiled lobster, Jonas," Sergeant Timothy Weatherly said as he placed his mug down on the newspaper. "What troubles you?"

"I...I just found the body of Emily Huggate half way along Snuff Mill Lane," Jonas said.

Inspector Leonard Pearson attended the scene in the company of Constable Herbert Wells and Dr Arthur Doyle.

After the doctor confirmed that the woman was dead, the inspector walked around the body and then hunkered down and saw the two red-rimmed holes in the corpse's neck.

"What do you make of *them*?" Leonard said to Dr Doyle. "Has she been bitten by some animal?"

"If that is the case, then it was an animal that I have not had the misfortune to come across," Dr Doyle said as he placed a finger and thumb across the space of the two holes. "It would appear that she was bitten deeply in her jugular vein, and the punctures are over two inches apart. There is no beast that I am aware of that could make such wounds, unless a wild creature originally from foreign lands has escaped from a city zoo and is roaming free."

The autopsy that followed was alarming. The late Emily Huggate was almost totally bereft of blood, and yet there had been none at the scene, and Dr Doyle had found no other injuries.

After two days had passed, Inspector Pearson had interviewed all the locals that had been in the Carpenter's Arms on that fateful night. Jimmy Pullman, a young man who worked at the nearby mill, had seen Emily walk out from behind the bar, to presumably leave the tavern to take a break from the smoke, sweat and stale ale smells that pervaded the pub. Jimmy had been in rowdy company, and had not noticed whether Emily had returned or not, but had seen the sinister old author, Edwin Morton, get up from a table soon after and leave the premises.

With no more leads to follow, Inspector Pearson drove out to Morton's house on the third morning after the slaying of Emily, to park his Wolseley at the bottom of wide stone steps that fronted the gravel-topped circle driveway. He was accompanied by his sergeant.

"Mister Morton is not to be disturbed," the housekeeper that opened the door said, after Leonard had informed her of his identity and asked to see her employer. "He is very old and is unwell and has taken to his bed."

"I'm sorry to hear that," Leonard said. "But this is a murder inquiry and we need to interview him."

"I shall tell him that you have paid a visit, and will ask him to call in at the police station this evening, if he is recovered enough to make the journey."

There was no reason for Leonard to argue the point: "Very well," he said. "But be sure that he understands the gravity of the situation."

Edwin drove into town at a few minutes after sundown, to park his Bentley in the yard at the rear of the police station. He walked around to the front and entered so quietly that Sergeant Weatherly was unaware of his presence until the brass desk bell, not six inches from his hand, was rung. He had been reading a report of stolen sheep from Bowman's farm, which was out near the windmill on the road to Heath Hill.

"Apologies if I startled you, officer," Edwin said as, open-mouthed, the policeman stepped back as if he had been stabbed with a knife. "My housekeeper informed me that Inspector Pearson wished to interview me."

Sergeant Weatherly swallowed hard, nodded, and went through a door behind him to where the inspector's office was located.

"The old man from Carlton Manor is out front, guv," the sergeant said. "He gives me the creeps."

"Show him through, Tim," Leonard said. "This shouldn't take more than a minute or two. I have no doubt that he is not implicated with what happened, but need to consider each and every possibility."

On entering the room, Edwin removed his fedora and said, "Good evening Inspector. How do you imagine that I can be of service to you?"

"Take a seat," Leonard said. "I trust that you are feeling much better than when we spoke with your housekeeper this morning."

"I am indeed. It was probably something I ate that made me unwell."

"Would you care for a cup of tea?"

"Thank you, but no. I have much work to do, and at my great age I acknowledge that time and tide wait for no man."

"I am advised that you are an author of some standing," Leonard said. "May I inquire as to what genre you write about?"

"In the main I produce historical tales of love and war, that for the most part dwell on the actions of both heroes and cowards. They are all factual, with just a touch of embellishment to keep a reader turning the pages. But my writing is not why you have summoned me here Inspector, is it?"

"No, it is with regard to the unnatural death of the young woman whose body was found on Snuff Mill Lane."

"I was told of it," Edwin said. "I believe that she was the daughter of the Carpenter's Arms landlord. He must be devastated by the loss."

"I assure you that he is, sir. Can you shed any light on what happened to the girl? For when she stepped outside the pub for a little fresh air, which I am to believe was a regular habit, you were seen to leave the premises, and could have been the last person to see her alive."

"If a foul deed was done to her, then surely the perpetrator of it was the last person to see her alive. I merely tipped my hat and bade her good night as I walked across the street to my car."

"Was she in the company of someone else?"

"Not that I noticed. She appeared to be alone."

"Very well," Leonard said. "Thank you for calling by."

"You are most welcome. I am by nature a little reclusive, but that does not mean that I do not care for the community at large. I wish that I could have been more helpful."

They shook hands, and Leonard was taken aback by both the icy coldness of the man's hand and the steely grip that he applied. And before Edwin turned to take his leave, Leonard saw a momentary shift in the man's face. For just a fraction of a second the wrinkled face seemed to become younger, and the coal-black eyes sparkled unnaturally, and the long white hair appeared to both thicken and darken, and he felt a sensation of vertigo. But no, in a flash the writer looked his usual age and self. It must have been a trick of the light, or overtiredness on his part.

A week passed, and Leonard contacted other constabularies and discovered that several other bloodless corpses had been found with what appeared to be bite marks to the neck. The overall opinion was that a giant snake was at large in the countryside and had bitten them, even though no venom was detected during the post-mortems. The only clue had been the discovery of a black fedora hat at one of the scenes.

Edwin Morton wore that kind of hat, Leonard thought. Could it be that there was a lot more to the old man than met the eye? He would call on him again and ask his whereabouts on the dates that other women had died by the same means. The man could have used some sort of two-pronged fork to commit murder, but that did not explain the blood loss. It was a mystery. None of the women had been sexually assaulted, and three had been carrying purses that had not been emptied of money.

Accompanied by Constable Wells, Leonard drove out to Morton's house, to knock at the door and once more be confronted by the housekeeper.

"We are here to see your employer," Leonard said to the stocky, middle-aged woman.

"Then I am sorry to disappoint you, Inspector," she said. "For he has driven down to London to some convention of writers, and I do not expect him to return for at least three days."

"Fine," Leonard said. "Be so kind as to write down the address of where he is staying."

"I did not ask him for it. It is not my place to question him. Had he wanted me to know, then he would have told me."

"I am advised that your name is Martha Clegg," Leonard said. "And I propose to ask you some questions, either here or in more formal surroundings at the station. Which will it be?"

"Come in," Martha said. "But be advised that I am a loyal servant to Mr Morton and will not say anything that would blacken his character."

Martha led them through to a large kitchen at the rear of the house, invited them to be seated, and then asked if they would like a cup of tea. They both declined.

"Mr Morton spoke of your conversation, Inspector," Martha said. "He had the feeling that you suspected him of having been somehow involved in the unfortunate death of Emily Huggate, though I cannot for the life of me understand why you would think that a man of his advanced years would or could be in any way implicated."

"How many wide-brimmed black fedora hats does he own?" Leonard said.

Martha frowned. "Four or five, I suppose. Does that have any relevance?"

"It could have. One such hat was found a short distance from where another woman was discovered with the same fatal injuries as Emily Huggate. It had a few long white hairs on it that cause us be at very least suspicious. We have times and dates that Mr Morton will be asked to provide an account of his whereabouts, before we can eliminate him as a suspect."

"Would you like to hear the truth of the matter, Inspector?" Martha said with a crooked smirk on her face that was bereft of any humour.

"Of course," Leonard said. "Any light that you are able to shed on the affair will be much appreciated."

"Then listen up and listen well. Edwin is much more than a distinguished writer. He is a being who has existed for over four hundred years. He is not what you believe him to be."

Leonard could not help but smile.

"Yes, smile Inspector, while you still can. The beauty of his status is that folks like you do not consider vampires to be real. They have all read wild tales, including that of the now mouldering idiot Bram Stoker, and think of vampires as mere scary flights of fancy that are fearful of garlic, signs of the cross and holy water. It is also believed that they show no reflection in mirrors, sleep in earth-filled coffins by day, and can be killed by sunlight or a wooden stake driven through the heart."

It was more than nonsensical to Leonard. The woman was obviously touched in the head, and yet she may know something of Edwin Morton that would offer up reason to replace suspicion of the man with some hard evidence with which they could act upon and arrest him.

"So you are stating that Mr Morton is a vampire?" Leonard said. "And that he murders by night, growing fangs to bite his victims' throats with, to drain them of blood."

"That is the truth of it," Martha said. "He is one of the undead that walk among you mere mortals, unrecognised for what they really are."

"Do you have any proof of this?" Leonard asked as he decided that the woman belonged in a lunatic asylum.

The air temperature in the kitchen suddenly plummeted, and the flames of the coal fire in the hearth dwindled and died as the woman that they thought to be Morton's housekeeper became indistinct and began to change, to shapeshift into the likeness of Edwin Morton; not ancient and infirm-looking, but a much younger man, *or vampire*, good-looking, with smooth if still pale skin, and ink black hair.

Time seemed to stand still. Leonard watched horror-stricken as Morton's hand shot out as quickly as a lizard's tongue will to snap up an insect, and witnessed what were now long and horny talons at the ends of the vampire's fingers sink through the coat and shirt of the constable, to punch through skin and flesh and rip free his beating heart.

Herbert Wells made a gurgling noise and stared wide-eyed at the pulsating organ in the creature's hand, and then looked down to the gaping hole in his chest, before slumping forward on the chair, for his face to drop down against the tabletop with a dull thud of finality.

Leonard made to move, but Morton raised his free hand palm up and said, "Stay exactly where you are, Inspector."

He was at once paralysed, not by fear alone, but by some numbing weakness that he believed was caused by the hypnotic stare that Morton was fixing him with.

Placing the now still and glistening heart on the table, Edwin glided around it to where Leonard was sitting. The vampire's mouth was open wide disclosing his teeth, the canines of which were now three times longer than that of an average person's, and as sharp as butchers' knives.

Leonard awoke in total darkness, feeling somehow hollow and without sense of fear or any other emotion. He had obviously suffered a vivid nightmare, for what he remembered as having happened was too fanciful to be true.

There was a scratching sound, and a sudden glare that he closed his eyes tightly against. When he opened them again, a soft yellow light from an oil lamp illuminated his surroundings. He was lying in a bed other than his own, and sitting next to it in a wingback chair, blowing out a match, was Edwin Morton.

"You have gone through a transition, Inspector," Edwin said. "To become much more than you have ever been before. I decided that you should not be sucked dry and discarded like a blood orange, but instead be turned, to become one of my kind. You are now one of the living dead; a vampire."

Rising up on his elbows with great difficulty, Leonard said, "But—"

"There are no buts, Inspector. You must come to accept that some things cannot be modified. You are at the beginning of a great journey, and will come to enjoy the powers and longevity that go hand in hand with it."

DAY OF RECKONING

FOSTER left his flat in Leyton, picked up the A113 and proceeded to drive north to Chipping Ongar. He was in no hurry, so stopped at a pub halfway to his destination and enjoyed a bar meal and a pint. Life was good. He got paid a lot of money to hurt or kill people, and it was all tax free.

By the time he reached the cottage it was dark. He parked on the grassy verge of a deserted B road, tight up against the bushes. Low tree branches whipped against the bodywork of the Cherokee. He turned off the ignition and lights, lit a cigarette and waited a couple of minutes before climbing out of the 4x4 and walking a further twenty yards to the open gateway. The track beyond it led to a small ramshackle cottage in a clearing that was choked up with weeds and overlong grass. There was an old Vauxhall parked outside the front door, and a light on at a downstairs window. He cautiously looked in through the grime-coated glass, past the partly open curtains to where he could see Davy Collins sitting in front of a big screen TV, holding a can of beer in his scrawny hand.

He smiled. He'd done his homework. Collins was a loner. There would be no one else in the house. Stepping to the door, he could see that it was loose in the frame, and that the wood was almost rotted through at the bottom. One solid kick next to the lock sent it flying backwards as the jamb disintegrated.

Davy jumped up from his chair, dropping the still half full can as he ran across the room to where a loaded shotgun was leaning in the corner near the kitchen door. He almost made it.

"Pick it up and I'll shoot you," Foster said. "Your call."

Davy froze, and then slowly turned and let his shaking hands fall to his sides. The stranger in front of him was tall, broad, and wore a long dark coat over shirt and tie. He looked like a stockbroker or financial advisor, but in his right hand he held a pistol with a silencer fitted to the end of it.

"Go and sit down again, Davy."

Davy did. He walked through the pool of beer that was slowly soaking through the greasy and almost nonexistent pile of the carpet, and was unmindful of the cold and sticky sensation on the soles of his bare feet as he sat down and said, "Who are—?"

"Doesn't matter who I am," Foster said. "All that matters is that you were skimming a little coke off Mr Chandler; too much for just your own habit. What I want to know is the name of who you sold it to, and where the money you were paid is."

Davy shook his head. "I swear to God I don't—"

The gun made no more noise than that of a soft handclap, as the baffles in the silencer muted the blast. Davy jerked sideways off the chair, screaming as he hit the floor, to writhe around clasping his right leg with both hands. Blood gushed from between his fingers from the penny-sized hole in his now shattered kneecap. The exit wound at the back was much larger, and the leg was partially severed.

"Name and money, son," Foster said. "I didn't come here to listen to any bollocks, which is where the next bullet will go if you don't talk."

Davy talked. Gave up the name of the dealer that he had sold the coke to, and told the shooter that the money was in a large ziplock bag at the bottom of the waste bin in the kitchen, under the liner.

Foster went into the kitchen, found the money and returned to where Davy was attempting to crawl across to where the shotgun was. He smiled and unscrewed the silencer from the 9mm semiautomatic and placed both components in a deep pocket of his coat, and then picked up the double-barreled Remington, to break it open and check that it was loaded.

"Your day of reckoning has arrived, Davy," Foster said as he snapped the barrels closed and took aim at the young man's head. "Any last words before I send you on your way?"

"Only that shooting me in the leg and making me scream will have woken my girlfriend up," Davy said through gritted teeth. "Oh, and I own *two* shotguns."

Foster frowned. He had been told that Davy Collins lived alone. Perhaps the punk was bluffing, trying to buy time. But he should have searched the house and not assumed that they were alone in it.

He heard the metallic click of hammers being pulled back, and spun towards the door that led out into the hall, to see a young woman standing there. She was wearing an almost see-through nightie, and was pointing a sawn-off 12 bore at him.

Gina was a little high, due to snorting too much nose candy and supping large shots of neat vodka. Her eyesight was blurred. She could see two images of a big guy pointing a shotgun at Davy, so just aimed middle for diddle and pulled the front trigger as he twisted round to face her.

The cluster of heavy gauge steel pellets punched a grapefruit-sized hole in Foster's chest. He was blown backwards by the force, to hit the wall hard and slide down it.

Shit! There was no pain, yet, and he guessed that he would be dead before his brain assimilated the shock and let his nerves transmit the agony. He attempted to breathe, heard a whistling sound from his ruined lungs, and then tasted warm blood as it welled up and flowed from his wide open mouth. And then he was gone. It was *his* day of reckoning that had arrived, not Davy's.

Gina dropped the weapon and went to Davy. He was beginning to pass out. Blood was pissing out of his leg. What to do?

Unbuckling the belt he wore, she pulled it through the loops of his jeans and fastened it around his thigh and tied it as tightly as she could.

"Call for an ambulance and the police," Davy whispered as he fought to stay conscious. "And then hide the cash and any coke that's left."

Gina gave it some thought. She would make the call, but didn't want to hang around. For all she knew Davy was dying. And she had shot a man to death, and whoever had sent him to kill Davy might just target her now.

As the ambulance arrived at the house in the wake of two police cars, Gina was already five miles away, driving north in Davy's Vauxhall. She had wiped the sawn-off and placed it in Davy's hands. And the money and coke were in her large shoulder bag, under the passenger seat. Sometimes you needed to cut and run, start afresh and make your own luck.

HELD TO RANSOM

THE fat green spider had been there for at least as long as he had. It came out at dusk from a wide crack at the juncture of the ceiling and the left side of the far wall, no doubt in search of live prey. He'd never seen it catch anything. How long could arachnids go without eating? That was just one of a thousand questions he had asked himself to keep sane, but had no answer to.

Turning over onto his right side, Jeff closed his eyes and tried to escape into sleep, where not all of his dreams were of a troubled nature, although most of them were. But in some he was free, back in the States with his beloved wife and daughter in Philadelphia.

The first month had been the worst. It had taken him that long to adapt to the predicament he was in and become able to face it realistically. Acceptance was the key to any given situation. He was a prisoner, and could not escape from his heavily armed captors. His life was literally in their hands. They had threatened to kill him on at least six occasions, even going to the extent of staging a mock execution, telling him to kneel down, to subsequently push the barrel of a gun to the side of his head. Why would they do this to a stranger that they neither knew nor had any quarrel with? Yet another question to ponder. But having steeled himself to face death, he had in some way overcome a hurdle. These people had – to a degree – unwittingly conditioned him to the fact that he may not survive this ordeal. The state of overwhelming fear he had endured could not be maintained indefinitely. It was now a dull blade, leaving him more philosophical about life and death.

A cockroach walked across the thin and stained cotton cover of the straw-filled mattress, just an inch from his face. He ignored it. A little later he sat up and listened. He could hear voices coming from another room in the building; even the laughter of a child. This was a group with an agenda. They hated him because of where he came from, not for who he was as an individual. It was politics. These terrorists used whatever methods they could to fight against a much more powerful enemy. They did not concede that might was right, or that they should be accepting of outside forces which impacted on their lives.

Looking at the bare, damp wall in front of him, he no longer counted the bricks. He knew that there were twenty-one rows, with an average of eight to a row, making a total of one hundred and sixty-eight. And the low-ceilinged room was almost square, so there were probably just under seven hundred bricks in all, allowing for the door. There was no feature of his small universe that he was not cognizant of.

Jeff Brody had left the downtown Radisson hotel at ten a.m. on June fifteen, exactly three months ago, to be snatched off the sidewalk in broad daylight: just bundled into the back of a van, to vanish without trace. He had not considered himself to be a potential target, although he was aware that groups did infrequently kidnap westerners, and so took all due precautions, not venturing out at night, or frequenting areas that the authorities decreed unsafe. His reasoning was that there were plenty of politicians and many other people that were high profile and therefore far more likely to be kidnapped. He'd been wrong. They had obviously seen him as a soft target.

As the CEO of a small but lucrative machine parts manufacturer, Jeff had established many contacts in the Middle East, and had not associated himself with any faction in particular, believing that to appear apolitical was the safe route.

The first few days of his incarceration had been a living nightmare. He had been kept blindfolded and trussed up, and told that he was to be filmed having his brains blown out. After time went by the blindfold and the plastic tie that bound his wrists together were removed. He now had a chain cuffed to his ankle that was attached to the wall.

Jeff knew that his life was well and truly on the line. He'd seen how some victims of radical organizations were held for varying lengths of time, and then put to death. And he also knew that the policy was not to concede to their demands. He had always agreed with the view that paying ransoms could only exacerbate the problem. But that was before *he'd* been taken. Now he had done a U-turn in his way of thinking. Call it selfish, but when it came to push or shove it was human nature to survive at all costs. He had once read of how a man on a sinking ferry had climbed over others, including women and children, to save his own skin. Jeff had been mortified at the time, sitting in his kitchen, sipping coffee, as far away from danger as he could imagine. But in the same circumstances would he have sacrificed himself for total strangers? Maybe not. This present situation had taught him not to stand in judgment over others; not unless you'd walked a few miles in their shoes.

There was a rap at the door. Jeff jumped to his feet and faced the wall, nose up against the brickwork, hands on top of his head, fingers laced. That was the rule. They'd got him acting like a trained dog. At first he had tried to be uncooperative, but a jolt from some kind of stun gun had convinced him that compliance was the only sensible course of action. Like it or not he was subjugated to their will. That hurt. But he'd had to swallow his pride, set it aside and let commonsense prevail.

"You are to be moved," a heavily accented voice said from behind him. "Lie down on your stomach and put your hands behind you."

Jeff was a big man. He had boxed at school and never backed down to anyone in his life. But he obeyed orders instantly now. He'd struggled when they'd first manhandled him into the back of the van, and the beating he had subsequently suffered was a learning curve. He had been kicked and punched until he was senseless, and had passed blood for a week, and thought that his kidneys might be seriously damaged.

Within seconds his wrists were bound, and a hood was in place over his head. Heart pounding, actually aching in his chest, Jeff wondered if this was it. Were they going to kill him and dump his body at the side of the road, as they'd boasted that they had done to the last hostage they had taken? Or had his ransom been paid? He could not allow himself to be optimistic. Pessimists had a point; if things went wrong they weren't as disappointed as folk that thought of the glass as being half full.

He was taken outside. It was cold. Nighttime. He was only wearing a now filthy sweat and blood-stained shirt and trousers. His feet were bare, and sharp stones dug into his soles. Big deal! That was the least of his worries. A vehicle's door was opened, and he was once more lying on gelid metal, perhaps in the same van that they had originally used to snatch him.

The journey could have taken ten minutes or ten hours. Jeff no longer had any proper perception of passing time; had learned to somehow open a door in his mind, step through it and escape from reality. Perhaps he was going insane. He had even enjoyed lengthy 'conversations' with his father, who had passed away over a decade ago. It was hard to know if he was hallucinating or dreaming. It didn't matter. He had found a parallel universe within himself, in which he could avoid the horror of his predicament. And his faith had proven to be crucial. Funny. He hadn't been to church – apart from attending weddings, funerals and a couple of christenings – since being a kid, and yet without consciously giving it a lot of thought, he had always known that there had to be more to life than he was aware of with his five senses. He had questioned God, one on one. Asked Him why, if He was indeed merciful, He would let this and all other atrocities take place. The answer was not immediately forthcoming. But it did come.

He realized that all men were made equal, but that free will gave them choices. Some made good ones and followed a righteous path. Others gave in to evil, to be corrupted and travel a crooked road. No one said living was easy. As he now knew, the passage through life was a series of trials.

The vehicle came to a halt, the back doors squeaked open, and he was helped out. Someone untied his wrists, and his hands pounded with pain as blood flooded back into them.

"This is where it ends, Mr. Brody," a gruff, monotone voice that held no quality of humanity said.

Jeff sank down to his knees and conjured up the image of his wife's and daughter's faces. Heard them tell him that they loved him. "I love you both, too," he whispered in reply.

"You are free, Mr. Brody," a voice said. "Stay where you are. We will make a call and you will be found. Do you understand?"

Jeff nodded his head, but did not believe what he was being told. It was no doubt a cruel trick. He imagined that he was about to be shot, and hoped that it would be quick and painless. A part of his mind almost welcomed the relief that a bullet would bring him.

Doors slammed, and the vehicle was put in gear and began to move away. Jeff stayed on his knees until the engine noise faded. Then still waited. All he could hear now was the desert wind, and feel grains of sand peppering him.

Slowly raising his hands, he gripped the bottom of the hood and pulled it up and off his head, to look around with his eyelids almost closed against the sand. He was in a desolate location. The wind subsided a little, and he could see low dunes stretching away on either side, looking ash-gray under the full moon that hung bright and pristine in a star-studded sky. It was a beautiful sight. One that, like so many other things, he had always taken hardly any notice of. At that moment he promised himself never to take anything for granted again. Every second should be cherished and not squandered.

Sitting on the soft sand at the side of the road, Jeff waited. A long time passed, but it was quality time, giving him the much needed respite to come to terms with his sudden change of fortune, and to reflect on what really mattered and was important to him.

Bright pinpricks appeared on the horizon, to grow and become beams that he recognized as being the headlights of vehicles.

Jeff began to laugh with nervous relief, and was still laughing when the first police car pulled to a stop next to him.

SOMETHING VERY STRANGE

THE full moon had risen to cast flat and cheerless shadows on the rutted earth of the narrow lane. Tall trees stirred in the chill wind, their branches soughing and the remaining life-sapped leaves rustling with the dry rasp of bronchial old men tittle-tattling on park benches.

Nick could make out the black shape of the pitched roof and chimneys silhouetted against the backdrop of a star-spangled sky. He paused for a few seconds; felt that the house was in some way aware of his approach. The skin of his scalp and forearms tightened, causing hairs to spring erect. He had the absurd feeling that the Victorian dwelling was leaning towards him, eager for him to draw nearer and be assimilated into its very fabric.

I don't want to go in there, he thought, experiencing an irrational stab of fear. In his mind, the house that loomed ahead of him had taken on a life of its own; something that existed on unholy ground. He felt sure that even had he possessed a crucifix, bible or holy water about his person, they would have offered little protection against the evil that emanated from the timeworn bricks and mortar. A fertile imagination produced terrifying images of undead figures in his brain; deformed and staggering stiff-legged, outstretched arms and long, white grasping fingers reaching forward, intent on latching onto him. Ignoring the crushing, unfounded fear, he slipped over the waist-high wall and approached the house in a crouching run, to make his way around to the back door, jemmy it open and step into the heavy, cloying silence, needing all his strength of will to dismiss the sensation that he might be crushed into nonexistence. The fleeting urge to turn back passed as quickly as it had come. The night was his friend; an ally in his unlawful pursuit.

Nick's girlfriend, Glenda, had been Silas Merrick's housekeeper for the last six years of the old man's life, and knew that he hoarded his pension and other money in the house. Now, with Silas dead and it being highly unlikely that anyone knew of his secret stash, Nick felt that he would be nothing short of remiss, should he not attempt to liberate it and put it to good use.

Silas had spent much of the last twelve months a virtual invalid, all but bedridden, and had no doubt kept his money close by. It would be upstairs, somewhere in the bedroom he had passed away in. Most people kept their valuables upstairs, seemingly unaware that it was the first place that any half-decent burglar would look.

Nick tiptoed through the large kitchen, out into the wide, oak-panelled hall, which in turn led to the staircase. His heart thudded, and cold sweat filmed his body. It was an unwarranted state to be in. He knew that there were no alarms, and that the house was unoccupied, yet he was overly apprehensive.

The creak of a complaining stair under his foot made Nick gasp and stand stock-still. His gloved hand ached with the force he was unconsciously gripping the banister rail with. He listened, but could hear nothing. But he *should* have heard something. The buffeting wind was surely strong enough to rattle the old sash windows, cause the gutters and down pipes to reverberate within their rusted brackets, and gain access through gaps to send draughts darting through the maze of sparsely furnished rooms. Instead, he might have been in a vacuum. Even the groan of the stair was unnaturally stifled, smothered and cut short.

Nick had the impulse to turn tail and run; to not stop until he was back amongst the streetlights at the end of the winding lane. All his instincts were imploring him to quit the creepy house, but commonsense and greed overrode his predisposition to retreat. He continued on up to the first landing, to where the bedroom he sought was situated. A window at the far end allowed a grainy brushstroke of light to illuminate it dimly. There were gilt-framed sepia photographs hung on the wall, and the faded wallpaper above them curled down from damp and crumbling plaster. Nick could smell the stale mustiness of the house; a palpable and pervasive sweet and sour odour that reminded him of mouldering oranges, tacky, grime-laden carpets, and the unseen and corrupting carcasses of rats in dark corners of attics. He would have to hurry, before his resolve snapped like an over-stretched rubber band.

Opening the second door on his right, he entered. The room was large and only contained: a bed, chest of drawers, wardrobe, and an armchair facing the window.

He determined to look in the obvious places first. He went across to the bed, lifted the mattress at first one side and then the other. There was nothing. The drawers were next. One by one he pulled them out, emptied the contents onto the patchwork quilt and sorted through them. There was nothing of value. Only the wardrobe left. It was a massive piece of furniture. Solid oak, he thought. Opening both the doors he was faced with a rail packed with suits and coats at one side, and shelves and drawers the other. The wardrobe's interior stank of mothballs. He emptied the drawers first. There was a gold wristwatch, but it was inscribed on the back, so he left it. Some of the cufflinks he found were probably of some value, so he took them. But where was the cash? He rifled through the pockets of jackets, trousers and coats, but they were empty. The thought of having to search the entire house was a daunting prospect. Every minute inside it was one too many. He couldn't shake off a sense of foreboding.

It was beneath the cluttered heap of shoes on the floor of the wardrobe that he found the old man's cache. The bottom board was canted up a little. He withdrew a penknife from his pocket, slipped the blade under the raised edge and prised it loose. In the space beneath lay a plastic supermarket carrier bag. He pulled it out, hurried over to the bed and tipped out the mass of bank notes. Yeesss! There was perhaps ten thousand pounds. He stuffed the money back into the bag, not inclined to count his newfound fortune in such an inhospitable environment. He would do that at leisure, back in the safety of his flat.

It was then that the temperature inexplicably dropped by at least twenty degrees. Each breath he exhaled turned to vapour, and he was at once chilled to the bone and began to shiver uncontrollably.

Clutching the bag full of his ill-gotten gains, Nick rushed to the door. Hadn't he left it open? It was now firmly closed. He twisted the now frost-covered brass knob and pulled. The door was stuck…Or locked. He felt panic grip him. It was as if a solid ball of ice formed in his stomach, and he began to make a strange whimpering sound. *Get a grip. It's not locked, just jammed. The wood must have swollen over time.* He dropped the carrier bag and used both hands in an attempt to pull the door loose from the clinging jamb. It did not budge. He kicked at it, even though he knew it opened inwards towards him, and that it was made of solid timber and would not break. Only when his foot hurt did he stop and try to rationalise his position and find some composure. It was no big deal. He would climb out of the window, hang from the sill and drop to the ground.

Walking back across the room, skirting the lone chair, Nick placed the bag on the floor, unlatched the window and pulled it up to look out. He grinned. There was a drain pipe fixed to the wall within easy reach. He would be out of this spooky house in seconds.

The window plunged down like a guillotine blade onto the backs of his hands, breaking several of his fingers. He screamed out, almost overcome by fear and pain in equal measure, and elbowed the glass, intent on breaking the window and dropping down into the bushes below. He was only on the first floor; it would be easy. And he had no choice, not with his fingers broken and swelling up.

The pane of glass seemed to have elastic properties. It might have been translucent rubber. It bounced back and regained its shape when he withdrew his elbow. He fumbled his knife out again; the bag of money now forgotten on the carpet at his feet. Gritting his teeth against the pain in his hands, he slashed at the window and was astounded to see that the rents he made in it appeared to heal up almost instantaneously.

Something very strange was happening. *Try the door again*, he thought, and turned...to be faced by the figure of Silas Merrick sitting in the armchair.

Nick could not move. Like a rabbit frozen in the path of a car's headlights, he could only stare open-mouthed into the face of a person who he knew for absolute certain was dead and buried. The old man was wearing a shroud, and his gaunt face was bloodless and ashen. The milky cauls of his eyes held no expression, and yet Nick knew that he was being examined, judged, and would no doubt meet some terrible fate for attempting to steal the dead man's money. His brain seemed to short circuit at the sight of a fat, black-backed beetle exiting from between the apparition's lips, to scuttle up and vanish into a nostril. It was all too much to bear.

Nick felt a crushing pressure in his chest, like a thick band of steel tightening and compressing it. He couldn't seem to move or think or breathe. And then the old man smiled, and he somehow found the strength to scream.

It was David Shadwell – who was handling the estate of his late client, Silas Merrick – who found Nick. He walked through the open door of what had been Silas's bedroom to find the body of the would-be thief lying supine on the carpet, between a dusty armchair and the window, of which the bottom pane was shattered. David was distressed by the look of absolute terror frozen on the corpse's face, and perplexed at the sight of a grubby carrier bag on the floor next to it, from which a large amount of bank notes had spilled out. Rushing out onto the landing, he reached into a pocket, withdrew his mobile phone and called the emergency services.

David did not even see the large black beetle that had dropped down from the chair, to be crushed under his foot as it headed for the nearest skirting board.

THE CASE OF THE HOBOKEN HANGMAN

I'M just plain Jack Lomax now, living in a double-wide on a trailer park at Port Orange, just a tad south of Daytona Beach on Florida's Atlantic coast. I was an officer and then homicide detective with the Hoboken Police Department for over twenty-five years, and have now been retired for a decade, and am used to folk asking me about the job. And in particular about the more lurid and gruesome aspects of the cases I worked. I can understand the morbid curiosity and fascination. TV series', books and movies exploit the dark side of people's nature. After all, murder makes for good mystery and intrigue. I enjoy watching stuff like CSI myself, even if I do smile and wonder how come any bad guys are still on the street. The show makes it look as if no one can kill and get away with it. Not true.

I looked on my work as purely investigative; to follow the trail of evidence, extrapolate clues and apprehend the perps. Not that it's always that simple. Sometimes there are no leads, no suspects and no physical evidence, such as a weapon, fingerprints, hair or fiber samples, DNA or a witness. The truth is that the majority of homicides are committed by persons known to their victims, and in many cases family members. It's most commonly an unpremeditated spur of the moment act, carried out due to rage or jealousy. It's the stranger-on-stranger killings that are harder to get a handle on and square away.

Where's all this hot air leading, I hear you say as I pull the tab on another can of Bud? Why is a retired cop putting his thoughts down on paper? Maybe because I spent so many years filling in reports of one kind or another, and need to tell my story. But no, that's not the whole truth of it. My wife, Sylvia, is at the mall, and I've just been sitting in the shade in the backyard, drinking too many cold ones and listening to the radio. It was reported on the top of the hour news that Carl Marston had died in prison – of natural causes – after serving over twenty-three years of a life sentence for the murders of three elderly women. Do you remember the case? He was nicknamed the Hoboken Hangman. Does that ring a bell? And yeah, I was the cop who brought him to book. Now let's be clear on this, there will be no gratuitous violence or many grisly details in the retelling of the case; 'Just the facts, ma'am', as Jack Webb used to say in his role as Joe Friday in the original Dragnet TV show. Yeah, I know, that dates me. Anyhow it isn't so much the people who were involved, but the events themselves that made this such an interesting and baffling case. Carl Marston nearly got away with it. I like to think I made a difference. Hell, I know I did. It might be best to see it through the eyes of the young and still wet behind the ears detective I was way back then. Why not come back with me and experience it from the horse's mouth, so to speak? Be at the crime scene and immerse yourself in a real 'whodunit', not a work of fiction. If you like a seemingly unfathomable mystery, then pour yourself a cup of java, or get a cold one from the refrigerator, find a comfortable chair and join me outside a rundown apartment block in Hoboken, in the days before most crimes could be solved in a laboratory.

With my lieutenant chain-smoking and stinking up the unmarked Ford, I drove into the parking lot fronting Liberty House. Pulled in next to a couple of cruisers and the ME's station wagon.

"This sounds like a straight forward suicide, Jack," Lt John Swift said, climbing out of the car, flicking open his Zippo to light another Winston, and side-stepping one of the many piles of dog crap that littered the weed-filled strip of grass between the curb and sidewalk.

"It's the same MO as the last two," I said. "Whoever does it wants us to believe that these old girls' are doing themselves in."

"We'll see. I'm not convinced."

Walking into the building, we both groaned at the sight of the 'out of order' signs taped to both of the graffiti-covered elevator doors.

"Jesus H. I'll probably have a heart attack before we get up to the tenth," 'Swifty' – as everyone at the precinct called John – grumbled as we headed for the stairs.

I took it slow. Even stopped and waited as my lard-assed boss came to a halt on the sixth floor to place his podgy hands on trembling, meaty thighs, with his head hulked down between his shoulders as he wheezed and fought for breath. Once recovered, he fired up another cigarette before moving onwards and upwards, bypassing discarded hypos and used rubbers.

"What've we got?" I asked the uniform outside the door of 1003.

The patrolman shrugged. "Not a lot. We had to break in. The door was locked from the inside, dead bolted with the chain on."

"Who called it in?"

"The guy in the apartment above this one. He hadn't seen the old broad for a few days, or heard her TV. And then he started to get a bad smell that wasn't coming from his garbage disposal."

I never did get used to seeing the deceased, or not feel sick to the gut from the stink the ripe ones gave off.

Ethel Palmer was in the kitchen, hanging from a pair of knotted pantyhose that had been tied off to a water pipe that abutted the wall and ceiling. On its side on the floor beneath her were her shoes and a ladder-back chair. I looked into the glazed, milky eyes of the dead senior citizen, noted all the other ghastly physical signs, and felt a combined flood of anger and sadness. That her life should have ended so violently was a tragedy.

"Anything for us to be interested in?" Swifty asked the medical examiner.

"Not that I can see, John," Dr. Dan Phelps said. "No sign of foul play."

"Did she leave a note?"

"No. But the majority of suicides don't. You know that."

While they talked I checked the apartment. The kitchen and living room were the only rooms with windows. Access had not been through them. They were both securely locked. I was almost convinced that the ME was right, and that this was no more than it appeared to be. But something was wrong. Call it a hunch. I wasn't certain that she had died by her own hand, even though there seemed to be no explanation other than the obvious.

Back in the kitchen I looked from the suspended corpse to the floor. Did mental calculations.

"I don't think the chair was used," I said.

Swifty and the ME stopped talking about the Monday night game and stared at me as if I'd grown a second head. I was a rookie to them. Just a fresh faced young guy with a new, shiny detective shield, but no credibility, yet.

Wearing latex gloves, Dan lifted the chair and positioned it upright under the human chandelier's bare, blue feet. The horny toenails dragged across the polished wood seat.

I was right, and we all knew it. There was no way that Ethel Palmer could have stood on tiptoe, applied the makeshift noose and then kicked the chair away. Leant up in the corner against the wall was a walking cane, and that made me doubt that Ethel could have even climbed up onto the chair under her own steam. The scene had been staged to allay suspicion. The chair was a prop. But whoever had murdered Ethel had not taken care of the fine detail. If more proof were needed, it turned up at the precinct the next day in the shape of Charlotte Coombes, the deceased's sister, who had traveled down from the Catskills to formerly identify the body and make the necessary arrangements.

"Ethel was a God fearin' Christian, who'd never dream of sinning by taking her own life," Charlotte sniffled through a soggy handful of Kleenex.

"Did you see much of her?" I said.

Charlotte nodded. "Bob, my husband, drove me down once a month, come rain or shine. We were at the apartment last weekend. And we made plans for Thanksgiving, so don't give me any shit about her doing such a terrible thing to herself. She was going to get out of this roach-infested dump and come to live with us. She was proud, didn't want to be a burden, but it was getting too much for her here. She had hip replacement surgery last year, and if the elevators were out she was stuck like a cat up a tree and had to rely on neighbors to get her essentials from the local market."

"Will you come to the apartment with me, now?" I said. "It would help if you could tell me if anything is missing."

Charlotte didn't stop crying for a second, but searched the apartment with the skill of a seasoned cat burglar. I stayed in the kitchen with her husband, who made a pot of fresh coffee. He offered me a cup, but I said I was fine. In my mind's eye I could still see Ethel suspended, purple-faced, with her tongue hanging out like a razor strop, and flies having themselves a feast.

"She didn't trust banks," Charlotte said when she'd finished scouring every nook and cranny. "She kept her cash in an old hatbox at the back of the closet in her bedroom. It's gone, and so has all her decent jewelry."

"Thanks," I said. I felt my stomach jumping. This was all the proof I needed to proceed. Ethel *had* been murdered.

"Don't thank me, sonny," Charlotte snapped. "Just find the evil sonofabitch who...who—"

"There, there, honeybunch," Bob Coombes said, hugging his junk food-fat wife to him. "Sit down and have a cup of coffee. The police will catch whoever did this to Ethel."

I wondered how? Although we now had a break. Charlotte could give a description of the missing jewelry, and if the killer tried to sell it, we might get lucky; like I might win the lottery. But there was still a big question screaming out for an answer. How had the perp gained entry to a tenth floor apartment that was locked up drum tight from the *inside*?

Later that day, after the Coombes' had listed the missing property and given statements, I went back to Liberty House. I was a detective, Goddamnit! There was a conundrum to find an answer to, and that was what I got paid poorly to do.

It only took me a few minutes to discover how the killer had managed to perform what seemed the impossible. And I also found a clue that gave us the means to track him down.

Now, even all these years later, I still take a certain amount of pride in having solved the case of the Hoboken Hangman. I know that if Carl Marston had not been captured, then he would have undoubtedly carried on robbing and murdering defenseless elderly women. Protect and Serve might sound corny, but it's what every good cop tries to do.

'Okay', I hear you say. 'Stop blowing your own damn trumpet ex-Detective Lomax and explain how Marston left the apartment, if all normal means were secured from within. Did he crawl through a ventilation duct'?

No. I'll tell you how he did it. He left in much the same way as any competent magician would vanish from a locked and chained cabinet or curtained cubicle; by way of a secret trapdoor. In Marston's case, it was through the wall into an untenanted apartment adjoining Ethel's. At some time, perhaps when his intended victim was out shopping or spending an afternoon at the local movie theater, he – being the superintendent at Liberty House – had let himself into the empty apartment and simply smashed through the thin bedroom wall, to wait for her return. The poor woman, with security in mind, had arrived home and unwittingly locked herself inside with a ruthless killer. After staging the hanging and finding the money and jewelry, Marston had cleaned up the debris, gone out through the hole and reached back in to maneuver Ethel's wardrobe up tight against it. With a criminal's overconfidence, he had been sure that it would be deemed a suicide, pure and simple. He would have repaired the wall before the apartment was leased again. But Ethel had been house proud. One confetti-sized piece of plaster drew my eyes to a deep indentation in the carpet, to the left of where the wardrobe had originally stood for many years.

Enough! I can hear the growl of the muffler on the Dodge. Sylvia has just pulled up outside, so I'd better go help with the bags. Where does time go?

Oh, I almost forgot the proof that led to Marston's downfall. It was nothing more than a very small piece of material snagged on a sharp outcropping of the manmade hole in the wall, which was later matched to a pair of his work coveralls.

I hope you enjoyed the insight into just one real-life solved crime. Maybe I'll put pen to paper again when I have an hour or two to indulge in reverie and look back on the career of the young detective who I used to be. I recall a serial killer who used to weight his victims' eyes closed with silver dollars, and always left a red rose in one of their hands. Turned out to be a wacko who hated his mother, and worked off his anger by murdering look-alikes. But that's another story from back in the day in Hoboken, New Jersey; the location of the first recorded game of baseball, and where the late crooner Frank Sinatra was born.

ALL THAT GLISTENS

THE ambulance and police arrived in tandem at 'The Priory', summoned by a hysterical maid who met them in the driveway, crying and unable to speak coherently.

Lady Helen Devere was already dead. Her body lay crumpled at the foot of the staircase, and the unnatural angle of her head led to an almost immediate presumption that she had fallen down the stairs and broken her neck. Only later, when it was found that a large diamond ring was missing, did the police begin to investigate the possibility that a murder had been committed in furtherance to an act of theft.

"Did she fall, or was she pushed?" Mrs Keast said the next day, as she noticed her employer reading the account in the newspaper.

Harry Greengrass looked up, his clear grey eyes peering over the top of his spectacles. He smiled, shrugged his shoulders a little, but offered no viewpoint.

An old man now, Harry had returned to his birthplace; the village of Little Cranston in North Yorkshire, wishing to see out his days in relative peace and quiet. His mind was not blunted, though, and writing his memoirs kept him employed. At eighty-four, Harry realised that his life had been a rich and colourful tapestry, full of both interest and intrigue. He had a background of service in naval intelligence, followed by a career with the Met, which he had retired from over twenty years ago, having risen to the rank of chief superintendent. His only real sadness was that his wife, Martha, had died ten years previously. He liked to think that she had just gone on ahead and that she was waiting somewhere safe and special for him to join her.

"I'll take tea in the garden, Mrs Keast," Harry said, rising from his chair with the aid of a stout cane, which gave slight relief to his arthritic knee. "I feel this spring sunshine should be taken advantage of."

Making his way out through the French windows to the private, high-walled garden, Harry paused beneath a broad oak, oblivious to the buzzing insects and singing birds. The demise of his near neighbour, and the theft, which was now the fourth to be suffered by the small community in the past eight days, intrigued him. No clues as to the culprit's identity – who always struck in broad daylight – had been found, which Harry took as a challenge. The only item missing from The Priory had been a very expensive solitaire diamond ring. The intruder had, it was thought, climbed a sturdy, ivy-clad trellis to gain entry to the master bedroom through an open window, whereupon he took the ring from the dressing table of the late and lamented dowager.

The police surmised that the thief had been confronted, and panicking, had pushed the unfortunate woman down the stairs in pursuance of making good his escape. As in the other three robberies, the rural 'Raffles' had gained access by way of upstairs windows that had been left open. Fortunately, no one else had been harmed, or had even been aware of the trespasser until they discovered that an item of jewellery had gone missing. It was thought that a local thief was responsible, who would probably not strike again, having been responsible, even if unintentionally, of taking a life.

"Drink it while it's hot, Mister G," Mrs Keast shouted, placing a tray on the cast-iron garden table and filling a cup from the fine bone-china pot.

Harry waved absently to his housekeeper and limped across the lawn; the fire in his knee demanding that he sit for awhile to take the weight off it.

The old ex-copper had lost maybe two stone in the decades since his active working life had come to an end, and his once smooth, round face was visibly thinner, its surface mapped with deepening furrows. His clothes, dark and funereal old friends, looked a little shabby and loose-fitting now, as did the shapeless, narrow-brimmed trilby that covered hair that was silver, where it had not deserted his mottled scalp. Sighing, Harry sat and sipped his tea, as for the hundredth time he considered the dilemma that had forced its way into his mind and demanded his attention. On one level this was akin to a tricky clue in a Times crossword; cryptic, thought provoking and initially baffling, but becoming clearer as many avenues were explored and subsequently discounted. His brain, in all matters, perused probabilities, narrowing the field of any problem down until only logical and possible solutions remained. He would then decide on a resolution that in most cases was the correct one. He would root out the perpetrator of these crimes. Of that he had no doubt.

Ben Briggs was the landlord of The King's Arms, and had been in-situ as such for almost eighteen years. He now stood at the window of the snug bar and watched, both fascinated and curious as the small black-suited figure moved across the village green, to stop and apparently make notes at the gates of The Priory. After a minute, the old man walked away, only to stop again to repeat the process outside Badger Cottage; another scene of recent robbery. In all, and within sight of Ben's hostelry, the retired copper surveyed the exteriors of all four crime scenes, and then, as though now satisfied, made a beeline across the green towards the pub.

"Nice to see you out and about, Harry," Ben said. "It must be a few months since you called in for a pint."

"I stay very close to the fireside throughout winter these days," Harry said. "Old age and thin blood go hand in hand, and encourage self-imposed confinement."

"So, what will be your pleasure?" Ben said, returning to his post behind the bar.

"I think that a large brandy and a soft seat by the window would be just the ticket," Harry said, tired now from an excess of fresh air and more walking than he had attempted in several years.

"I couldn't help but notice," Ben said as he pushed the glass up to the optic. "But you seemed to be taking notes at the front of all the properties that were robbed. I don't wish to appear ill-mannered or to be prying, but my curiosity is aroused."

"Well, Ben," Harry said, smiling as he took the balloon glass, swirled the amber contents around and sniffed them before taking a sip, to find the mellow warmth a rare pleasure. "If you don't ask, you won't find out. The truth is, I don't like to be confounded by the unexplained, and so I am investigating this little crime spree of ours. I've just been putting a theory to the test, and wondering if the piece of jigsaw I think fits, does."

"And does it?" Ben said as Harry inhaled the strong bouquet of the brandy again and took a deep, satisfying draught, licking his lips and replacing the empty glass on the bar top with a noticeably palsied hand. His alert stare, alive with undimmed enthusiasm, made contact with his host. And behind that piercing, slightly unnerving gaze, Ben could see the metal of the man inside, who now, outwardly, was suffering from the relentless march of time.

"Oh, yes, Ben. I feel that I may soon have a name to identify the guilty party," Harry said with a mischievous smile playing on his lips. "I should think that by tomorrow I will have all the proof I need to warrant giving Sergeant Travers a call. He can take full credit and show these city detectives how it's done."

"Old Harry Greengrass is on the blower, sir," the constable said, his hand over the receiver as he frowned at Sergeant Charlie Travers. "He's asking to speak to you. What shall I tell him?"

"Yes, Harry. What can I do for you?" Charlie said, snatching the phone from the PC, a little annoyed that the youngster – who hadn't even been a twinkle in his dad's eye when Harry Greengrass was putting villains away – could only think of the ex-copper as an old man.

"No rush, Charlie," Harry said. "But when you have a spare minute or two, pop round for a cup of tea, and I'll tell you who committed the robberies and was responsible for Lady Devere's demise."

Charlie could get no further information over the phone, and was in his car and driving to Harry's house within a minute of hanging up.

"Good morning, Charlie," Ethel Keast said as she opened the door to the man who she had known since he had been a little snot in short trousers. "He's out back, sat in the sun and looking like the cat that's got the cream."

Harry would not be rushed. He made idle chitchat until Mrs Keast served them with tea and then retreated back inside to the kitchen. Only then did he begin his longwinded exposition of the events in question.

"You're saying that you purposely left a first floor window open, and then placed a gold ring and a pair of cufflinks on display?" Charlie said.

"Yes, Charlie, I did. It's a fact that at the other four houses, only a single item of jewellery was removed. And in each case an open window was the point of entry."

"Yes, yes, we know that, Harry. What point are you making? What, if anything, can you tell me that I don't already know?" Charlie said, becoming a trifle impatient and wondering why he was humouring the once highly respected copper, who was now perhaps just a mite senile and eccentric.

"The ladders by my greenhouse," Harry said. "Would you place them up against that oak tree, and then indulge me by climbing up, say twenty feet."

Feeling more than a little foolish, Charlie climbed up into the leafy canopy. And then he saw it; a large ill-made nest of twigs, with a magpie sat in it, staring at him with emotionless oil-bead eyes. Startled, the avian thief screeched and flew off, to settle on the chimney stack of a nearby cottage.

"How did you work it out, Harry?" Charlie asked as he placed the stolen items he had recovered from the nest onto the tabletop.

"I noticed that the bird had taken up residence in my oak just before the first robbery. They are notorious collectors of bright objects, and so when I left my bait and it took it; case closed. Lady Devere must have disturbed the blighter as she reached the top of the stairs, and in turn she was badly startled and probably stepped back and fell as it most likely screeched and flew up off her dressing table with the diamond ring in its beak."

Later, after Charlie had gone, Harry went inside for a nap. He was feeling a tad smug. It may not have been the crime of the century, but he had solved the riddle of Lady Devere's untimely death, and shown these young coppers that he could still outthink them if he put his mind to it.

A HEAVY HEART

FROM where Danny lay, unable to move, he could see through the large window, but was not looking out to what was beyond it, his mood being reflective and his lacklustre eyes unfocused. Was it...could it really be over a dozen years ago that he had unintentionally and in an instant committed such a dreadful act, that had altered the course of his and other people's lives so irrevocably? It was bizarre how something that could happen in just a fraction of one lousy second in a person's life became a benchmark; the sole criterion by which people came to judge you. Single acts could become historic for good and bad reasons, or be instantly forgettable. One thing was for sure, what is, is. Years of wishing you could throw the dice again was a pointless exercise. He had decided that everyone carried a millstone over something, and would like nothing better than to go back and do some things differently. But ifs, buts and regrets didn't alter a damn thing. Life was a one-off performance; a ticket to ride the ultimate rollercoaster. You'd got to hold on tight, go with the flow, and make it through the peaks and troughs the best that you could, unable to walk away until the car came to a stop.

God! Time was dragging. He knew all about time. It was elastic; could stretch to become drawn out and almost interminable. Or contract, shrink and petrify, compressed into the briefest of moments. Fluid like a river, time can flow by sluggishly, silted up, creeping with the tardiness of molasses. Or race, a raging torrent, swift, tumbling, blurring the senses in its pell-mell rush.

Life and the abstract of time cannot be simply measured in seconds, days, years or millennia. It passes and is gone, but can seem to telescope to eternal dimensions or vanish in a trice, depending on the individual occupation that accompanies it.

Time is beyond comprehension, intangible and without form or substance. It is apart from all that dwells within its incorporeal non-existence; a figment of imagination, contrived by sentient life forms whom are sadly aware of their own mortality, and insist on acknowledging their passing by marking the duration of their transient, supposed existentialism.

Yes, that was a real mouthful. He was now far more erudite than he had been in his youth. And he was obsessed with time, and chose to view it as an ethereal commodity that he likened to sand cascading through an hourglass. He was running out of it, down to the last few grains, and allowed himself to go back for the millionth time and review what had happened; the act that had led him on the inevitable path to where he now was.

At first he had been angry, not contrite in the least. It wasn't his fault. He hadn't asked to be born. And if he had, it wouldn't have been into a slum area of Washington DC. Or to an alcoholic, out of work father, and a mother who subsidized their welfare check by standing on street corners, wearing boob tubes and leather skirts that barely covered the assets she was offering to punters.

He – Danny Martin – had not been afforded the chance to ever be more than he became. If there was blame to be attached, then surely it belonged fairly and squarely on the shoulders of his parents, society, and the world in general. He was a product of poverty, his color, and the way things were. Had he been born to middle-class white parents in some well-to-do suburb, then things would have been vastly different. He was a victim of circumstance. It was that simple. He knew what mean streets were; had fought on them, and learned the craft of survival in the human jungle. But now, with the benefit of hindsight, if he could relive that long gone December evening, then he would not be on his way to oblivion. He didn't want to go back and replay it. But it was like a loop of videotape. For twelve years it had gone round and round. He continually edited it, changed the script in his mind to alter the outcome; to make things turn out for the better.

Danny let his mind run with the uncut version of what had *really* transpired in that liquor store on the corner of Rockville and Wheaton; although the whole picture was not available to him. Had it been, he would have known that Officer John Kelly was nearing the end of his shift on that bleak Christmas Eve and was looking forward to spending the holiday with his family. For the first time in several years he had two full days off, and had just used his coffee break to do some last minute shopping, picking up one or two additional gifts for his wife, Helen, and son, Patrick. He would, he thought, wrap them when he got home, while enjoying a large shot of Irish whisky.

On his way back to the precinct, John reached for the pack of cigarettes on the unit's dash, only to find it empty. Having run out, he wanted a smoke even more. He thought that the craving made him a 'sad' man, but it highlighted what addiction to anything can do to you. All he could think of was getting another fix. With some people it was booze, with others coke or heroin, and for millions, like John, tobacco. The dependency was a need that overrode all other considerations, to the point that an urgent staccato voice repeated and insisted with growing intensity that he must have a cigarette, and *now*. The voice of reason said, ease up, you're not a freakin' junkie, you can do without. But he was, and he couldn't.

Angling the cruiser through lead-gray slush, John stopped outside a liquor store, nerves already relaxing, knowing that he would be firing up a Marlboro in just a minute or two.

Stepping inside the door, he forgot all about cigarettes as he assimilated the scene in front of him. He had walked into an ongoing armed robbery. The old guy behind the cash register looked to be the owner. Blood from a deep gash above his left eyebrow was running down his cheek into a thick beard, turning it from white to crimson. Facing him over the counter was a young black punk with a mass of dreadlocks, who looked to be no more than eighteen. Next to him, farther from John, helping himself to Hershey bars and other candy was an even younger youth.

John drew his police special as his brain processed every detail. His main and most immediate concern was the nickel-plated Saturday night special that 'Dreadlocks' was waving in the air in front of the shaking owner's face. The teenager turned to face John, wild-eyed and agitated.

The bullet hit him in the chest, quickly followed by two more in his stomach. *Jesus and Mary, the kid can shoot*, John thought, driven back into the door as he pulled the trigger of his own gun.

The bullet from John's .45 tore through the teenager's right arm, hitting bone, to be deflected and exit, to shatter a bottle of Southern Comfort on a wall shelf. Blood splashed over the second boy's face and chest, causing him to throw himself backwards away from it, which saved his life as John fired again; the hot lead displacing the air where a fraction of a second earlier the kid's head had been.

The younger robber curled up on the floor in a fetal ball, next to his wounded companion. John warned them both not to move, and then told the owner to dial 911.

The .22 caliber pistol had not had the stopping power to put John down. But with the situation under control, his legs gave way, and he dropped into a sitting position with his back up against the wall.

"Get me a cigarette, wouldya?" John asked the ashen-faced owner, Brad Walker, who had now been robbed three times in six months and was seriously contemplating selling up and moving to the wilds of Montana, or even Alaska.

John managed one deep drag from the lit cigarette that Brad placed between his lips before drifting into the black.

At the hospital, Patrick and his mother were perched on the edge of green plastic contour chairs at John's bedside. The internal damage caused by the three slugs had given surgeons little chance to save his life. The massive internal hemorrhaging could not be controlled. Like a dam with cracks widening under pressure, the force of the deluge tore and pushed, filling body cavities, extending the fissures until the whole structure collapsed, overwhelmed by the volume of liquid.

Father Murphy administered the last rites, while in numbed shock, Helen held her dying husband, whispering tearful words of love as he began to convulse. Finally, as his muscles relaxed, his body straightened out and appeared to arrange itself neatly on the bed. With a long expiration of breath that sounded for all the world like a melancholy sigh, John died. Both Patrick and his mother held their breath, waiting for him to take another gulp of the antiseptic hospital air, only breathing again when blood forced open the corpse's mouth, to run down onto the pillow and spread like a port wine stain on the white linen.

From Danny's point of view it was definitely not his fault. He and Clifford Curtis had been robbing the liquor store, and couldn't deny it. But nobody would have got wasted if the dumb cop hadn't walked in and drawn his gun. Danny viewed it as self defense, pure and simple. He'd taken a shot in the arm and almost died. But all that was history. Now, he saw it from a different perspective. Hell, with so many years on death row under his belt, he'd had time to revaluate. The man he now was had little in common with the hoodlum he had been back then. He'd learned to read and write, and had become a better person; even contacted the cop's widow, not to try to elicit forgiveness, but just to admit his guilt, apologize unreservedly, and acknowledge that he had done a terrible thing.

It was time. Through the window he looked out at the solemn faces of those that had assembled as silent witnesses to his final moments. Funny, it didn't feel like justice was being done. Strapped to a cruciform-shaped gurney with a needle and IV line in his arm was cold-blooded murder – albeit legal – in his book. But he felt ready. There was no fear left in him, just relief. He was completely penitent and contrite for his past actions. He smiled, knowing that the sodium pentothal would put him to sleep painlessly, and that he would be mercifully unaware when the pancuronium stopped all muscle activity, including his respiration, preceding the potassium chloride which would still his heavy heart.

A TERRIBLE PLACE

TATE hit the platform on the run and leaped through the doors as they began to close, to stumble forward and crash into a suitcase almost as big as the woman standing guard over it.

The train was packed, rounding off what had conspired to be a God-awful day. He wished he'd driven into the city, but had opted to avoid the stress of bumper-to-bumper traffic. Big mistake.

Three stops and forty minutes later, he got a seat. Sank back into it and closed his eyes. Was almost lulled to sleep by the rhythm of the swaying coaches, when his bladder demanded that he relieve it.

Some things are just so utterly bizarre that the mind finds it hard to grasp the reality of them and has to do a double-take to check out that which cannot, or has no right to exist. That happened to Tate when he closed the door, engaged the bolt and turned as he reached down to unzip his pants.

He froze at the sight that met him. The back wall of the cubicle, which was the side of the coach, was missing. Beyond the stainless steel toilet and basin there was a gaping hole in the train. Not a ragged rent, but a rectangle of obsidian blackness; a doorway framed by lichen-spotted granite columns that supported a broad and timeworn lintel. And there was no sound. He could no longer hear the wheels of the train singing on the rails, or feel any sensation of movement.

Tate's eyes were drawn to the deeply incised letters on the crumbling stone; Terribilis est locus iste. Terribilis translated to terrible, he could figure that much out. And this was more than terrible. This was Twilight Zone stuff. His usually agile mind could not comprehend what was happening. He was a down-to-earth, meat and potato kind of guy who had never given any credence to the supernatural and other associated weird shit. He saw things in simple terms: black and white, night and day, good and bad, and life and death. And this was not anything like any situation he had experienced and could relate to. He was baffled, at a loss to know what to do next.

Backing away, he fumbled the bolt off and left the small compartment with the sensation of an ice-cold wire of fear snaking down the length of his spine. He was no longer just tired and annoyed, he was bemused, and panic was threatening to confuse him further.

Running between what were now deserted seats, he made it to the buffet car, and entered. He could smell coffee, the lingering scent of perfume, and even a trace of sweat in the air. But the car was now, as the rest of the train, unoccupied. There was a full glass of beer on the counter. He sat on a stool and took a mouthful of the cold liquid. It tasted sulfurous. He spat it out.

Calm down. Study the facts, Tate mused. He had caught the night train, and other passengers besides him had been on board when it left the last stop. People do not just vanish, and alien abduction was strictly for the movies. So where were they?

As if in answer to a silent prayer, the uniformed woman who had been serving coffee and tea appeared through the far door of the car and made her way through another door next to the counter.

"Hello," he called. "Excuse me. I need to ask you something."

No reply.

"Hey, get the hell out here, right now," he demanded. She had no idea who she was dealing with. Had she known that he was a professional hitman who had no sense of compassion and did not feel a shred of guilt or remorse over the dozens of marks he had eliminated, then she would be more than eager to show him some respect.

The woman appeared and stared at him impassively.

Jesus! Tate recognized her. She was a dumpy middle-aged redhead with a band of freckles across her plump cheeks and small pug nose. And her mouth was a downward curving slash. He slid off the stool, took three paces backwards, only stopping when he came up against the side of the carriage.

Her eyes were bulging, spotted with blood. He knew that this was petechiae; small pinpoint hemorrhages that signified asphyxia. It was something he had seen many times, due to a penchant for strangling his nominated female victims.

He even remembered her name. This was Helen Mellor, a councilor who had vetoed an application for some building development that his gangland employer wanted to go through. She had been in the way, and had not had the sense to listen to fair warning or be bribed, and so ended up paying the ultimate price at his hand.

How could she be here?

"It wasn't personal," he said defensively. "I was just following orders."

The dead woman made as if to speak, but made the cawing sound of an enraged crow. The flex that was still embedded in her neck had fractured the cricoid; the ring-shaped cartilage of the larynx, making speech impossible.

Tate was shaking. He saw a dark stain erupt from the material of her uniform, over the flat side of her chest, from where he had sliced off the breast as a trophy.

It was at that moment the missing passengers began to return, to file into the buffet car and move towards him.

He must have gone insane, or suffered a stroke, or was experiencing the fucking mother of all nightmares. That was it! He was asleep. He just *felt* wide awake. He closed his eyes, counted to ten and opened them, to no avail.

Why had he not recognized them earlier? There was a woman who had been sat facing him, working a laptop. And a balding, middle-aged guy who'd been across the aisle, wearing headphones and tapping his fingers to unheard music. And a younger man who had been on a Smartphone. He had murdered all three of them.

Tate's nerve gave. He ran out of the buffet car, back down the aisle, only to be stopped in his pell-mell dash when he tripped over his own feet, to fall heavily, cracking his head on the arm of a seat. He sprang up, ignoring the blood that flowed down from his forehead to sting his eyes as he reached up to pull the emergency stop handle. He braced himself against the expected bite of steel on steel as the driver applied the brakes, but the train slid on smoothly through the slick, oily night.

There was no way out. Zombie-like corpses that had died in the grip of his glove-encased hands or by bullets from his gun, lurched towards him.

He was not beaten yet. The toilet with the entrance to a dark tunnel was only a few feet from him. He ran to it, went into the cubicle and locked the door behind him.

A sudden touch at his side caused him to cry out. No one was there. He reached into his jacket pocket and pulled out a ziplock bag. Within it, the severed thumb of the man he had murdered that day was flexing and twisting, trying to escape, its intention to somehow do him harm. And through the translucent plastic he could see the navy-blue tattoo of an eye on its lower knuckle...blinking rapidly, as if seeking him out to stare accusingly at him.

Tate screamed and hurled the bag into the toilet bowl and flushed it.

"Better get a grip, Mr. Tate," a deep, resonant voice said from the dark maw of the unnatural doorway in the side of the carriage. "You will need to ready yourself for much worse than this."

"Who...who are you?" Tate asked the apparition that materialized before him. "Where am I?"

"My name is Charon," the tall, shadowy figure said, slipping back the cowl of his cloak to reveal a skull that was pliable and could alter its expression. "And this train, not a boat, is your mode of transport to Hades."

On the lintel above the ghoul, Tate saw the engraved Latin letters shift and reform into English to spell out; *this is a terrible place.*

And so it was.

Tate was drawn through the hellish gateway, to be sucked into a world of physical and mental excruciation. He was surrounded by hordes of others who screamed and writhed under the horrendous suffering they were being subjected to by demonic torturers.

Tate had no way of knowing that he had been felled by a massive, fatal heart attack as he ran to catch the train. He had collapsed and died on the platform. But the circle of life goes on, and his future was to be one of abject wretchedness in purgatory. Atonement would gain no favor. This was not a place where redemption was an option. At the end of the day, you reap what you have sown, forever.

That's it folks

You've met a selection of seriously good and bad characters in the preceding short stories. I hope that you enjoyed coming face to face with some of them, and that the variety in the anthology kept you turning the pages. I based many of the murderers and other criminals on inmates that I came into contact with during my 20+ years in the Prison Service. But the bottom line is, it's fiction. I do my best to write entertaining yarns, bearing in mind that Abe Lincoln was right in saying, 'you can never please all of the people all of the time'. I write what my imagination feeds me with, and can only cross my fingers and be optimistic in thinking that you, the reader, found a few of them to your liking.

About The Author

I write the type of original, action-packed, violent crime thrillers that I know I would enjoy reading if they were written by such authors as: Lee Child, David Baldacci, Simon Kernick, Harlan Coben, Michael Billingham and their ilk. Over twenty years in the Prison Service proved great research into the minds of criminals, and especially into the dark world that serial killers - of who I have met quite a few - frequent.

I live in a cottage a mile from the nearest main road in the Yorkshire Wolds, enjoy photography, the wildlife, and of course creating new characters to place in dilemmas that my mind dreams up.

What makes a good read? Believable protagonists that you care about, set in a story that stirs all of your emotions.

If you like your crime fiction fast-paced, then I believe that my books will keep you turning the pages.

Connect With Michael Kerr and discover other great titles.

Facebook

www.facebook.com/MichaelKerrAuthor

Also By Michael Kerr

DI Matt Barnes Series
A REASON TO KILL
LETHAL INTENT
A NEED TO KILL
CHOSEN TO KILL
A PASSION TO KILL
RAISED TO KILL

The Joe Logan Series
AFTERMATH
ATONEMENT
ABSOLUTION
ALLEGIANCE
ABDUCTION

The Laura Scott Series
A DEADLY COMPULSION
THE SIGN OF FEAR

Other Crime Thrillers
DEADLY REPRISAL
DEADLY REQUITAL
BLACK ROCK BAY
A HUNGER WITHIN
THE SNAKE PIT
A DEADLY STATE OF MIND
TAKEN BY FORCE
DARK NEEDS AND EVIL DEEDS
DEADLY OBSESSION

COFFEE CRIME CAFÉ

Science Fiction / Horror
WAITING
CLOSE ENCOUNTERS OF THE STRANGE KIND
RE-EMERGENCE

Children's Fiction
Adventures in Otherworld
PART ONE – THE CHALICE OF HOPE
PART TWO – THE FAIRY CROWN

Printed in Great Britain
by Amazon